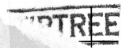

**Logan rounded ran straight into Rowan.**

Logan scrambled backward. "How—?" she started, before breaking off, her lips pinching closed, because of course he knew his way about the maze. It was *his* maze.

His castle.

His world.

Her eyes burned. Her throat ached. She'd struggled for so many years—struggled to provide and be a strong mother—and now it was all being taken from her. Her independence. Her control. Her future.

She didn't want anything to do with him and yet here he was, blocking her path, filling the space between the hedges, tall and broad, so very strong…

"What are you doing?" he asked.

"You've trapped me," she whispered, her eyes bright with tears she wouldn't let spill because, God help her, she had to have an ounce of pride. "You've trapped me and you know it, so don't taunt me…*don't*. It's not fair."

With a rough oath, he reached for her, pulling her against him, his body impossibly hard and impossibly warm as he shaped her to him. She shivered in protest. Or at least that was what she told herself when dizzying heat raced through her and the blood hummed in her veins, making her skin prickle and tingle and setting her nerves on fire, every one dancing in anticipation.

Her h

searc                                              nt of

softn

# The Disgraced Copelands

*A family in the headlines—for all the wrong reasons!*

For the Copeland family each day brings
another tabloid scandal. Their world was one of
unrivalled luxury and glittering social events. Now
their privileged life is nothing but a distant memory…

Staring the taunting paparazzi straight in the eye,
the Copeland heirs seek to start new lives—
with no one to rely on but themselves.
At least that's what they think…!

*It seems fame and riches can't buy happiness—
but they make it fun trying!*

Read Morgan Copeland's story in:
*The Fallen Greek Bride*

Read Jemma Copeland's story in:
*His Defiant Desert Queen*

Read Logan Copeland's story in:
*Her Sinful Secret*

# HER SINFUL SECRET

BY
JANE PORTER

First Published in Great Britain 2017
By Mills & Boon, an imprint of HarperCollins*Publishers*
1 London Bridge Street, London, SE1 9GF

© 2017 Jane Porter

ISBN: 978-0-263-92437-4

Our policy is to use papers that are natural, renewable and recyclable
products and made from wood grown in sustainable forests. The logging
and manufacturing processes conform to the legal environmental
regulations of the country of origin.

Printed and bound in Spain
by CPI, Barcelona

*New York Times* and *USA TODAY* bestselling author **Jane Porter** has written forty romances and eleven women's fiction novels since her first sale to Mills & Boon Modern Romance in 2000. A five-time RITA® Award finalist, Jane is known for her passionate, emotional and sensual novels, and loves nothing more than alpha heroes, exotic locations and happy-ever-afters. Today Jane lives in sunny San Clemente, California, with her surfer husband and three sons. Visit janeporter.com.

## Books by Jane Porter

### Mills & Boon Modern Romance

*Bought to Carry His Heir*
*A Dark Sicilian Secret*
*At the Greek Boss's Bidding*
*Hollywood Husband, Contract Wife*

#### *The Disgraced Copelands*

*The Fallen Greek Bride*
*His Defiant Desert Queen*

#### *A Royal Scandal*

*Not Fit for a King?*
*His Majesty's Mistake*

#### *The Desert Kings*

*The Sheikh's Chosen Queen*
*King of the Desert, Captive Bride*
*Duty, Desire and the Desert King*

#### *Desert Brides*

*The Sheikh's Disobedient Bride*

Visit the Author Profile page
at millsandboon.co.uk for more titles.

# CHAPTER ONE

"LOGAN, WE'VE GOT a crowd outside. *Logan*. Are you listening?"

Frustrated by yet another interruption, Logan Copeland tore her gaze from her script, yanked off her headset and glared up at her usually very capable assistant, Joe Lopez. She'd come to think of him as a genius and a blessing, but he wasn't much of either at the moment. *"Joe."*

"We've got a problem."

*"Another* one?" she asked incredulously. They were down to less than twenty-four hours now before tomorrow night's huge gala fund-raiser, the biggest of Logan's career, and nothing was going right in the tech rehearsal for the fashion show that would happen during the gala, and nothing would go right if Logan continued to be interrupted.

"We honestly don't have time for this. *I* don't have time for this. And if you want to run the show tomorrow on your own, that's fine—"

"I don't," he interrupted, expression grim. "But this is big, and I can't manage this one without you."

"Why not? And why does everything have to be a big problem right now?" she retorted, aware that every interruption was costing more time with the crew, which cost more money, which meant less money for the charity. "If this isn't life or death, you need to deal with it, and let me get one good run-through in before—"

"The media has descended. Full-on, out of control paparazzi stakeout. Here."

Logan's expression brightened. "But, Joe, that's great news. The PR team is succeeding. I heard they were the best. How is that a problem?"

"Logan, they're not here because of tomorrow's Hollywood Ball. They're not interested in the Gala or doing good. They're here for *you*."

Logan suddenly found it hard to breathe. She pressed the clipboard to her chest, headset dangling from her fingers. "For the press conference about the Ball," she said firmly, but then at the end her voice quavered, and the fear and doubt was there.

*"No."* Joe shoved his hands into his jeans pockets. He was a smart, young, artistic twentysomething just a couple years out of college, and he'd been invaluable to Logan since coming to work for her two years ago, a little over a year after her whole world had imploded due to the scandal surrounding her father, Daniel Copeland. Lots of people had wanted nothing to do with Logan after news broke that her father was the worst of the worst, a world-class swindler and thief preying on not just the wealthy, but the working class, too, leaving all of his clients nearly bankrupt, or worse.

Joe had grown up in a tough Los Angeles neighborhood marked with gang violence, so the Copeland scandal hadn't been an issue for him. He wanted a job. Logan needed an assistant. The relationship worked.

He, like everyone, knew what her father had done, but unlike most people, he knew the terrible price Logan had paid. In most business and social circles she was still persona non grata. The only place she could work was in the nonprofit sector. "They are here to see *you*," he repeated. "It's to do with your dad."

She stilled. Her gaze met Joe's.

His dark brown gaze revealed worry, and sympathy. His voice dropped lower. "Logan, something's happened."

The tightness was back in her chest, the weight so heavy she couldn't think or breathe.

"Have you checked messages on your phone?" he added. "I am sure you'll have gotten calls and texts. Check your phone."

But Logan, normally fierce and focused, couldn't move. She stood rooted to the spot, her body icy cold. "Was he freed?" she whispered. "Did the kidnappers—"

"Check your phone," a deep, rough, impatient male voice echoed, this one most definitely not Joe's.

Logan turned swiftly, eyes widening as her gaze locked with Rowan Argyros's. His green gaze was icy and contemptuous and so very dismissive.

She lifted her chin, her press of lips hiding her anger and rush of panic. If Rowan Argyros—her biggest regret, and worst mistake—was here, it could only mean one thing, because he wouldn't be here by choice. He'd made it brutally clear three years ago what he thought of her.

But she didn't want to think about that night, or the day after, or the weeks and months after that…

Better to keep from thinking at all, because Rowan would use it against her. More ammunition. And the last thing a former military commander needs is more ammunition.

He didn't look military standing before her. Nor had he looked remotely authoritative the night she met him at the bachelor auction fund-raiser to benefit children in war-torn countries in need of prosthetics. He'd been a bachelor. She'd helped organize the event. Women were bidding like mad. He would go for a fortune. She didn't have a fortune, but when he looked at her where she stood off to the side, watching, she felt everything in her shift and heat. Her face burned. She burned and his light green gaze remained on her, as the bidding went up and up and up.

She bought him. Correction: she bought *one night* with him.

And it only costs thousands and thousands of dollars.

The remorse had hit her the moment the auctioneer had shouted victoriously, "Sold to Logan Lane!"

The intense remorse made her nauseous. She couldn't believe what she'd done. She'd filled an entire credit card, maxing it out in a flash for one night with a stranger.

She didn't even know then what Dunamas Maritime was. Insurance for yachts? Ship builder? Cargo exporter?

He knew that, too, from his faint mocking smile. He knew why she'd bought him.

She'd bought him for his intense male energy. She'd bought his confidence and the fact that of all the attractive men being auctioned, he was by far the most primal. The most sexual.

She'd bought him because he was tall and broad shouldered and had a face that rivaled the most beautiful male models in the world.

She'd bought him because she couldn't resist him. But she hadn't been the only one. The bidding had been fierce and competitive, and no wonder. He was gorgeous with his deep tan, and long, dark hair—*sun-streaked* hair—and his light arresting eyes framed by black lashes. There was something so very compelling about him that you couldn't look away. And so she didn't. She watched him… and wanted him. Like every other woman at the charity event.

They'd all looked and wanted. And many had bid, but

she was the one who'd bid the longest, and bid the highest, and when the heart-pounding bidding frenzy was over, she came out the victor.

The winner.

And so, from across the room that night, he looked at her, his mysterious light hazel eyes holding hers, the corner of his mouth lifting, acknowledging her victory. Looking back she recognized the smile for what it was—mockery.

He'd dared her to bid, and she had, proving how weak she was. Proving to him how easily manipulated.

By morning he would hate her, scorning her weakness. Scorning her name.

But that hadn't happened yet. That wouldn't happen until he'd taken her again and again, making her scream his name as she climaxed once, twice and then, after a short sleep, two more times before he walked out the door the next morning.

The sex had been hot, so hot and so intense and so deeply satisfying. With anyone else it might have felt dirty, but it hadn't been with him. It'd just felt real. And right.

But she did feel dirty, later, once he'd discovered she wasn't Logan Lane, but Logan Lane Copeland, and the shaming began.

It was bad enough being hated by all of America, but to be branded a slut by your very first lover? A man that wasn't just any man, but one of the best friends of your twin sister's new husband?

Of all the people to sleep with…of all the men to fall for…why did it have to be Rowan Argyros with his passionate Irish Greek heritage and ruthless nature? There was a reason he'd risen through the military. He was a risk taker with nerves of steel. A man who seized opportunities and smashed resistance.

She knew, because he'd seized her and smashed her.

Logan exhaled now, blocking the past with its soul-crushing memories. She hated the past. It was only in the last year she'd come to terms with the present and accepted that there could be a future. A good one. If she could forgive herself…and him.

Not Rowan—she'd never forgive Rowan. It was her father she needed to forgive. And she was trying, she was.

"My father," she said now, her gaze sliding across Rowan—still so tall and intimidating, still so sinfully good-looking—and then away, but not before she realized his long hair was gone. Shorn. He looked even harder now than before. "Is…he…?"

Rowan hesitated for just a fraction of a second, and yet his expression didn't soften. "Yes."

She willed herself not to move, or tremble. She firmed her voice so it wouldn't quaver. "How?"

He hesitated yet again, and she knew that he knew every detail. He was a maritime antipiracy specialist, based out of Naples, with offices in Athens and London as well as a large country estate in Ireland. He hadn't told her any of that. Her sister Morgan and her husband Drakon Xanthis had, after their wedding.

"Does it matter?" he asked quietly, coolly.

"Of course it matters," she retorted, hating him even more. Hating him for taking her virginity and mocking her afterward for enjoying his body and touch and for leaving her to deal with the aftermath on her own, as if he hadn't been the one in that big bed with her…

His silence made her fear the worst. Her heart hammered. Her stomach fell. She wished she was hearing this from Morgan or Jemma, or her older brother, Bronson. They would all have broken the news differently. "Did they…did they…?"

And then she couldn't wait for the words, the confirmation that her father, kidnapped and held hostage off the coast of Africa, had been killed, possibly executed. It was all too sickening and her legs wobbled and her head spun, her body hot, then cold and then very cold.

She tried to look for Joe, the very best assistant one could ever hope for, but all she saw was Rowan and he was staring her down with those pale hazel-green eyes.

"Don't," he growled, his deep, rough voice now sounding far away, as if he was standing at the far end of a tunnel.

Maybe he was.

She couldn't see him well. Things were cloudy at the edges. He was cloudy, and she blinked, almost amused that Rowan could think he could still dictate to her, once again telling her body what to do...

"You're not doing this now," he snapped.

But she did. Her world went dark.

Swearing, Rowan dove to catch Logan before she crashed to the ballroom floor, but he was too far away and couldn't break her fall. Her head slammed on the edge on the stage as she went down.

He was there to scoop her up and he swore again, this time at himself, for not reaching her more quickly, and then at useless Joe, for not catching her, either.

She was still out cold as he settled her into his arms, her slender body ridiculously light. He shifted her so that her head fell back against his biceps, and his narrowed gaze raked her pale face, noting the blood pooling at the cut on her temple, and beginning to trickle into her thick honey-colored hair. She was going to have a nasty bruise, and probably one hell of a headache, later.

She was also still impossibly beautiful. High cheekbones, full lips, the elegant brow and nose of a Greek goddess.

But beauty had never been her issue. If she'd just been a pretty face, he could forgive himself for their night together, but she wasn't just a beautiful girl, she was Logan *Copeland*, one of the scandalous Copelands, and as amoral as they came.

It was bad enough being bought at a charity auction but to be paid for with embezzled funds?

"Grab her things," he told the man hovering at Logan's side. He wouldn't be surprised if Joe was Logan's lover. A boy toy—

He broke off, unable to continue the thought. He didn't like the thought. But then, he didn't like anything about being here today.

He didn't have to be the one doing this. He could have sent one of his men. Every one of his special ops team at Dunamas Intelligence had come from an elite military background: US Navy SEALs, British Special Forces, Russia's Alpha Group, France's National Gendarmerie Intervention Group, Spain's Naval Special Warfare Force. Rowan hadn't just interviewed and hired each, he'd then trained them personally for intelligence work and rescue operations.

Any one of his men could do what he was doing. He should have sent anyone but himself.

But Rowan wasn't about to let anyone else near her. He told himself it was to protect them—she was a siren after all—but with her in his arms, he knew it was far more personal and far more primal than that.

He didn't want any man near her because even three years later, her body belonged to him.

Logan struggled to open her eyes. Her head hurt. Her thoughts kept scattering. She was being carried up and up. They were moving, climbing, but climbing what? She could hear breathing as well as the sound of heavy, even thudding close to her ear. She was warm. The arms holding her were warm. She battled to open her eyes, needing to focus, wanting to remember.

She stared hard at the face above her, noting the jaw, a very strong, angular jaw with a hint of dark beard. He had a slash of cheekbone and a firm mouth. And then he looked down at her, and the sardonic hazel-green depths sent a shiver through her.

*Rowan.*

And then it started to come back. Joe saying there was a problem. Something with her father and then Rowan appearing…

She stiffened. "Put me down."

He ignored her, and just kept climbing stairs.

Panic shot through her. "What's happening? Why are you carrying me?"

She wiggled to free herself.

His grip grew tighter. "Because you fainted, and you're bleeding."

"I didn't."

"You did. You smacked your head on the edge of the stage when you fainted, probably have a concussion."

"I'm fine now," she said, struggling once again. "You can put me down. Now. Thank you."

"You won't be able to make it up the stairs, and we've got to get out of here, so don't fight me, because I'm not putting you down," he said shortly, kicking the door to the roof open. "And if you don't like being carried, then next time don't be clumsy. Faint somewhere soft."

"Where's Joe? I need Joe!"

"I'm sure you do," Rowan gritted as they stepped into

the dazzling California sunshine. "Don't worry, he's following with your things."

"My things? But why?"

"I'll fill you in once we're in the air. But enough chatter for now." His cool gaze dropped and swept from her face down her neck to the swell of her breasts. "You're not as light as you like to think you are."

But before she could react, they were at the helicopter and the pilot was jumping out and opening the door. Rowan was putting her in the helicopter in one of the passenger seats but she turned in his arms, leaning past to find Joe.

"Logan," Joe said, trying to reach her.

Rowan kept his arm up, blocking Joe from getting too close. "Put her things down," Rowan directed, "and step back."

But Logan grabbed Joe's sleeve. "Handle things at home, Joe. Please?"

Joe's dark eyes met hers and held. "Where are you going? When will you be back?"

"She'll call you," Rowan said drily. "Now say goodbye."

"Tomorrow's event," Logan said.

Joe nodded. "We'll make it work. I'll make it work. Don't worry."

And then Rowan was climbing into the helicopter and the pilot began lifting off, forcing Joe to run backward to escape the intense wind from the churning blades.

"Nice boy," Rowan said, shutting the door as Joe scrambled to safety. "Definitely on the young side, but so much more trainable before twenty-five."

Logan shot him a furious glance. "He's not my boyfriend."

"Your lover, whatever." He shrugged. "It's not for me to judge what you do with your father's money—"

"I don't have a penny of my father's money."

"I'm sorry. It wasn't his money. His embezzled billions."

She ground her jaw tight and looked away, chest aching, eyes burning, mouth tasting like acid. She hated him…she hated him so much…

And then he leaned over and checked her seat belt, giving it a tug, making the harness shoulder straps pull tight on her chest.

She inhaled sharply, and his fingers slid beneath the wide harness strap, knuckles against the swell of her breasts.

"Too tight?" he asked, his gaze meeting hers, even as her nipples tightened.

"With your fingers in there, yes," she choked, flushing, her body now hot all over. The linen and cotton fabric of her cream dress thin enough to let her feel everything.

He eased his hand out, but not before he managed to rub up against a pebbled peak.

And just like that memory exploded within her—his mouth on her breast, alternately sucking and tonguing the taut tip until he made her come just from working her nipple.

Her response had whetted his appetite. Not content with just the one orgasm, he devoted himself to exploring her body and teaching her all the different ways she could climax. It had been shocking but exciting. She'd been overwhelmed by the pleasure but also just by being with him. He'd felt so good to her. She'd felt so safe with him. Nothing he did seemed wrong because she'd trusted him—

Logan bit into her bottom lip hard to stop the train of thought. Couldn't go there, wouldn't go there, not now, not when her head ached and the helicopter soared straight up, leaving the top of the old Park Plaza Hotel building so quickly that her stomach fell, a nauseating reminder that she still wasn't feeling 100 percent.

She put a hand up to her temple and felt a sticky patch of blood. She glanced down at the damp crimson streaking her fingers, rubbed them, trying not to throw up. "I know you specialize in rescue and intelligence, but isn't the helicopter getaway a bit much?"

Rowan thrust a white handkerchief into her hands.

She took it, wiping the blood from her fingers, hoping she hadn't gotten any on her dress. This was a new dress, a rare splurge for her these days. As she rubbed her knuckles clean she could feel him watching her. He wasn't amused. She wasn't surprised. He didn't have a sense of humor three years ago. Why should he have one now?

"I just meant, it's a little Hollywood even for you," she added, continuing to scrub at her skin, feeling a perverse pleasure in poking at him, knowing he'd hate anything to do with Hollywood. Rowan Argyros might look like a high-fashion model, but she'd come to learn after their—*encounter*—that he was hardcore military, with the unique distinction of having served once in both the US Navy and the Royal Navy before retiring to form his own private maritime protection agency, a company her brother-in-law had invested heavily in, wanting the very best protection for his Greek shipping company, Xanthis Shipping.

Even more bruising was the knowledge that Morgan and Drakon were such good friends with Rowan. They both spoke of him in such glowing terms. It didn't seem fair that Rowan could forgive Morgan for being a Copeland, but not her.

"Look down," Rowan said tersely, gesturing to the streets below. The huge hotel, built in 1925 in a neo-Gothic style, filled the corners of Wilshire, Park View, and West Sixth Street. "That mob scene is for you."

Still gripping the handkerchief, she leaned toward the window which made her head throb. A large crowd pressed up against the entrance to the building, swarming the front steps, completely surrounding the front, with more bodies covering the back.

It *was* a mob scene. They were lying in wait for her. "Why didn't they go in?" she asked.

"I chained the front door. Hopefully your Joe will find the key, or he'll be in there a while."

Logan reached for her purse and slipped the handkerchief inside and then removed her phone. "Where did you put the key? Joe can't stay in there—"

"That's right. You've left him with instructions to manage things at home." He watched her from beneath heavy lids. "What a good boy."

She ignored him to shoot a quick text to Joe.

Rowan swiped the phone from her hands before she could hit Send.

She nearly kicked him. "Why are you so hateful?"

"Come on, babe, a little late now to play the victim."

Logan turned her head away to stare out the window, emotions so chaotic and hot she could barely see straight. "So where are you taking me?"

"To a safe spot. Away from the media."

"Good. If it's a safe spot, you won't be there." She swallowed hard, and crossed her arms over her chest. "And my father. He's really dead?"

"Yes."

She turned her head to look at him. Rowan's cool green gaze locked with hers, expression mocking. "If it makes you feel better," he added, lip curling, "it was natural causes."

Blood rushed to her cheeks and her face burned. Good God, he was even worse than she remembered. How could that be possible? "Of course it makes me feel better."

"Because you are such a dutiful daughter."

"Don't pretend you cared for him," she snapped.

"I didn't. He deserved everything he got, and more."

She hated Rowan. Hated, hated, hated him. Almost as much as she wanted to hate her father, who'd betrayed them all—and she didn't just mean the Copeland family, but his hundreds of clients. They'd trusted him and he'd robbed them blind. And then instead of facing prosecution, instead of accepting responsibility for his crimes, he'd fled the country, setting sail in a private yacht, a yacht which was later stormed off the coast of Africa—he was taken prisoner. Her father was held captive for months, and as time dragged on, the kidnappers' demands increased, the ransom increased. Only Morgan was willing to come up with money for the ransom…but that was another story.

And yet, even as much as she struggled with her father's crimes and how he'd shamed them and broken their hearts, she still didn't want him suffering. She didn't want him in pain. Maybe she didn't hate him as much as she thought she did. "So he wasn't murdered. There was no torture," she said, her mouth dry.

"Not at the end."

"But he was tortured."

His eyes met hers. "Shall we just say it wasn't a picnic?"

For a long moment she held her breath, heart thumping hard as she looked into his eyes and saw far more than she wanted to see.

And then she closed her eyes because she could see something else.

The future.

Her father was now dead and so he would never be prosecuted for his crimes, but the world still seethed. They demanded blood. With Daniel Copeland gone, they'd go after his five children. And while she could handle the scrutiny and hate—it was all she'd been dealing with since his

Ponzi scheme had been exposed—her daughter was little more than a baby. Just two and a quarter years old, she had no defenses against the cruelty of strangers.

"I need to go home," she choked. "I need to go home now."

Rowan had been watching the emotions flit across her face—it was a stunning face, too. He'd never met any woman as beautiful. But it wasn't just her bone structure that made her so attractive, it was the whole package. The long, thick honey hair, the wide-set blue eyes, the sweep of her brows, the dark pink lips above a resolute chin.

And then the body...

She had such a body.

He'd worshipped those curves and planes, and had imagined, that night three years ago, that maybe, just maybe, he'd found the one.

It's why he became so angry later, when he discovered who she was, because he'd felt things he'd never felt. He'd felt a tenderness and a connection that was so far out of his normal realm of emotions. What had started out as sex had become personal. Emotional. By morning he wasn't doing things to her, he was making love with her.

And then it all changed when he discovered the pile of mail on her kitchen counter. The bills. The magazine subscriptions.

Logan Copeland.

Logan Copeland.

Logan Lane Copeland.

It had blindsided him. That rarely happened. Stunned and then furious, he turned on her.

Many times he'd regretted the way he'd handled the discovery of her true identity. He regretted virtually everything about that night and the next morning, from the intense lovemaking to the harsh words he'd spoken. But over the years the thing he found himself regretting the most was the intimacy.

She'd been more than tits and ass.

She'd meant something to him. He'd wanted more with her. He imagined—albeit briefly—that there could be more, and it had been a tantalizing glimpse at a future he hadn't thought he would ever have. But then he saw it and realized that he wanted it. He wanted a home and a wife and children. He wanted the normalcy he'd never had.

And then it was morning and he was trying to figure out the coffee situation, and instead he was dealing with a liar-deceiver situation.

He wasn't in love. He wasn't falling in love. He'd been played.

And he'd gone ballistic. No, he didn't touch her—he'd never touch a woman in anger—but he'd said things to her that were vile and hurtful, things about how she was no better than her lying, crooked, greedy father and how it disgusted him that she'd bought him with money that her father had embezzled.

He didn't like remembering that morning, and he didn't like being responsible for her now, but he could protect her during the media frenzy, and he'd promised his friend and her brother-in-law, Drakon, that he would.

"There's no going home," he said tersely. "Your place must be a zoo. You'll be staying with me until the funeral."

Her blue eyes flashed as they met his. "I'm not staying with you."

"Things should calm down after the funeral. There will be another big story, another world crisis, people will tire of the Copelands," he said as if she'd never spoken.

"I have a job. I have clients. I have commitments—"

"Joe can handle them. Right?"

"Those clients hired me, not a twenty-four-year-old."

"I did think he looked young."

She lifted her chin, and her long hair tumbled over her shoulder, and her jaw firmed. "He's my assistant, Rowan. Not my lover."

"You don't live together?"

"No."

"Then why would you tell him to manage things at home?"

Her mouth opened, closed. "I work from home. I don't have an outside office."

"Yet he was genuinely worried about you."

She gave him a pitying look before turning to look out the window. "Most people are good people, Rowan. Most people have hearts."

Implying he didn't have one.

She wasn't far off.

His lips curved faintly, somewhat amused. Maybe if he was a teacher or a minister his lack of emotions would be a problem. But in his line of work, emotions just got in the way.

"The tin woodsman was always my favorite character," he said, referencing L. Frank Baum's *The Wonderful Wizard of Oz*.

"Of course he was," she retorted, keeping her gaze averted. "Except he had the decency and wisdom to want one."

# CHAPTER TWO

"So where are we going?" she asked as the minutes slid by and they continued east over the city. Los Angeles was an enormous sprawl, but she recognized key landmarks and saw that they were approaching the Ontario airport.

He was slouching in his seat, legs outstretched, looking at her from beneath his lashes, not at all interested in the scenery. "One of my places."

He acted as if he was so casual. There was nothing careless or casual about Rowan Argyros. The man was lethal. She'd heard some of the stories from Morgan after her night with Rowan, and he was considered one of the most dangerous men on the planet.

And she had to pick him to be her first lover.

Genius move on her part.

Although to be fair, he'd never touched her with anything but sensitivity and expertise. His hands had made her feel more beautiful than she'd ever felt in her entire life. His caress had stirred her to the core. It would have been easy to imagine that he cared for her when he'd loved her so completely...

But he hadn't loved her. He'd pleasured her because she'd *paid* him to, giving her a twenty-thousand-dollar lay.

She swallowed around the lump filling her throat. Her eyes felt hot and gritty as she focused on the distant flight tower. She didn't want to remember. She hated remembering, and she might have been able to forget if it hadn't been for the one complication...

Not a small complication, either.

So she regretted the sex but not the mistake. Jax wasn't a mistake. Jax was her world and her heart and the reason Logan could battle through the constant public scrutiny and shame. Twice she'd had to close her Twitter account due to Twitter trolls. She'd refused to shut down her Instagram, forcing herself to ignore the daily onslaught of scorn and hate.

She'd get through this. Eventually. The haters of the world didn't matter. Jax mattered, and only Jax.

"So which home are we going to?" she asked, trying to match his careless, casual tone, trying to hide her concern and growing panic. Jax's sitter left between five and six every day. Even if Joe went to the house to relieve the sitter, he was merely buying Logan a couple of hours. Joe had never babysat Jax for more than an hour or two before. Joe was a good guy, but he couldn't care for the two-year-old overnight. Knowing Joe, he'd try, too, but Logan was a mama bear. No one came between her and her little girl.

"Does it matter?" he asked, pulling sunglasses from the pocket of his jacket.

So very James Bond. Her lip curled. He noticed.

"What's wrong now?" he asked.

She glanced away from him and crossed her legs, aware that she could feel the weight of his inspection even from behind his sunglasses. "Morgan told me how much you love your little games." She looked back at him, eyebrow arching. "You must be feeling very powerful now, what with the daring helicopter rescue and clandestine moves."

"I do like your sister," he answered. "She's good for Drakon. And he for her."

Logan couldn't argue with that. Her sister had nearly lost her mind when separated from her husband. Thank God they'd worked it out.

"Hard to believe you and Morgan are twins," he added. "You're nothing alike."

"Morgan chose to live with Dad. I didn't."

"And your baby sister, Jemma, she just chose to move out, even though she was still a teenager."

Logan swung her leg, the gold buckle on her strappy wedge sandal catching the light. "You're not a fan of my family, so I'm not entirely sure why we're having this conversation."

"Fine. Let's not talk about your family." His voice dropped, deepening, going almost velvet soft. "Let's talk about us."

*Let's talk about us.*

Her entire body went weak. She stopped swinging her leg, her limbs suddenly weighted even as her pulse did a crazy double beat.

*Us.* Right.

She couldn't see his eyes, but she could tell from the lift of his lips that he was enjoying himself. He was having fun, the same way a cat played with its prey before killing it.

She could be nervous, show fear, try to resist him—it was what he wanted. Or, she could just play along and not give him the satisfaction he craved.

Which, to her way of thinking, was infinitely better.

She smiled at him. He had no idea who he was dealing with. She wasn't the Logan Lane he'd bedded three years ago. He'd made sure of that. "Oh, that would be fun. I love talking about old times." She stared boldly into the dark sunglasses, letting him get a taste of who she'd become. "Good times. Right, babe?"

For a moment he gave her no response and then the corners of his mouth lifted even higher. A real smile. Maybe even a laugh, with the easy smile showing off very white, very straight teeth. The smile changed his face, making him younger and freer and sexy. Unforgivably sexy. Unforgivably since everything inside her was responding.

Not fair.

She hated him.

And yet she'd never met anyone with his control and heat and ability to own a room…and not just any room, but a massive ballroom…as if he were the only man in the entire place. As if he were the only man on the face of the earth. As if he'd been made just to light her up and turn her inside out.

Her heart raced and her pulse felt like sin in her veins. She was growing hot, flushing, needing…and she pressed her thighs tighter.

No, no, no.

"We were good," he said, still smiling at her, and yet his lazy drawl hinted at something so much more dangerous than anger.

Lethal man.

She'd wanted him that night and the fascination was back, slamming into her with the same force of a two-ton truck.

Something in her just wanted him.

Something in her recognized something in him and it shouldn't happen. There was no reason for someone like Rowan to be her type…

"It was you," she said, feeling generous. And what harm could there be in the truth? Because he was good—very, very good—and he was making her feel the same hot bright need that she'd felt during the bachelor auction. And it'd been forever since she'd felt anything sexual, her hunger smashed beneath layers of motherhood and maternal devotion. "You have quite the skill set."

"Years of practice, love."

"I commend your dedication to your craft."

His dark head inclined. "I tried to give you value for your twenty grand."

She didn't like that jab. But she could keep up. He and the rest of the haters had taught her how to wrap herself in a Teflon armor and just deflect, deflect, deflect. "Rest assured, you did. Now, if I knew then what I know now, I might have given you a few pointers, but I was so green. Talk about inexperienced. Talk about *embarrassing*. A twenty-four-year-old virgin." She shuddered and gently pushed back a long tendril of hair that had fallen forward. "Thankfully you handled the old hymen like the champ you are."

He wasn't smiling anymore.

Everything felt different. The very air was charged, seething...pulsing...

She gave him an innocent look. "Did I say something wrong?"

Rowan drew off his sunglasses and leaned toward her. "Say that again."

"The part about the hymen? Or the part where I wished I'd given you a few pointers?"

His green eyes were no longer cool. They burned and they were fixed intently on her, laser beams of loathing.

She'd finally gotten a rise out of him. She had to work very hard to hide her victorious smile. "But surely you knew I was a virgin," she added gently. "The blood on white sheets...?"

"It wasn't blood. It was spotting."

She shrugged carelessly. "You probably assumed it was just from...vigorous...thrusting."

His eyes glowed and his square jaw turned to granite. "You weren't a virgin."

"I was. And don't you feel honored that I picked you to be my first?" She glanced down at her hands, checking her nails. She must have chipped one earlier, when she fainted and fell. She rubbed a finger across the jagged edge and continued conversationally. "You set the bar very high, you know. Not just for what happened in the bedroom, but after."

He said nothing and so she looked up from her nails and stared into his eyes. "I can't help but wonder, if I hadn't climaxed during each of the...sessions...would you still have called me a whore?" She let the question float between them for a moment before adding, "Was it the fact that I enjoyed myself...that I took pleasure...that made me a whore? Because it was a very fast transition from virgin to whore—"

"Virgins don't spend twenty grand to get laid," he said curtly, cutting her short.

"No? Not even if they want to get laid by the best?"

He'd stopped smiling a long time ago. He had a reputation for being able to handle any situation but Logan was giving him a run for his money.

If it were any woman but Logan Copeland, he'd be impressed and maybe amused. Hell, he'd been amused at the start, intrigued by the way she'd thrown it down, and given it right back at him, but then it had all taken a rapid shift, right around the time she'd mentioned her virginity, and he didn't know how to fight back.

She'd been a virgin?

He didn't do virgins. He didn't take a woman's virginity. And yet he'd done her...quite thoroughly.

Dammit.

"You're taking my words out of context," he said tightly, trying to contain his frustration. "I didn't call you a whore—"

"Oh, you did. You called me a *Copeland* whore."

He winced inwardly, still able to hear the words ringing too loud in the kitchen of her Santa Monica bungalow. He could still see how she'd gone white and the way her blue eyes had revealed shock and then anguish.

She'd turned away and walked out, but he'd followed, hurling more insults, each a deliberate hit.

He despised the Copelands even before the father's Ponzi scheme was exposed. The Copelands were one of the most entitled families in America. The daughters were fixtures on the social scene, ridiculously famous simply because they were wealthy and beautiful.

Rowan grew up poor and everything he had, he personally had worked for.

He had no time for spoiled rich girls.

How could shallow, entitled women like that respect themselves?

Worse, how could America adore them? How could America reward them by filling their tabloids with their pictures and antics? Who cared where they shopped or which designer they wore?

Who cared where they vacationed?

Who cared who they screwed?

He didn't. Not until he'd realized he'd screwed one of them senseless.

But it hadn't been a screw. That was the thing. It had been so much more.

Rowan's jaw worked. His fingers curled into fists. "I regret those words," he said stiffly. "I would take them back, if I could."

"Is that your version of an apology?"

It had been, yes, but her mocking tone made it clear it wasn't good enough. That he wasn't good enough.

Rowan wasn't sure whether to be offended or amused.

And then he questioned why he'd even be offended. He'd never cared before what a woman thought of him.

He'd be a fool to care what a Copeland thought of him.

"It is what it is," he said, the helicopter dipping, dropping. They'd reached the Ontario airport. His private jet waited at the terminal.

Her head turned. She was looking down at the airport, too. "Why here? Do you have a place in Palm Springs?"

"If I did, we'd be flying into Palm Springs."

"I find it hard to believe you have a place in Ontario."

"I don't." He left it at that, and then they were touching down, lowering onto the tarmac.

Rowan popped the door open and stepped out. He reached for Logan but she drew back and climbed out without his assistance.

She started for the terminal but he caught her elbow and steered her in the other direction, away from the building and toward the sleek white-and-green pin-striped jet.

She froze when she realized what was happening. *"No."*

He couldn't do this again, not now. "We don't have time. I refuse to refile the flight plan."

"I'm not leaving Los Angeles. I *can't.*"

"Don't make me carry you."

She broke free and ran back a step. "I'll scream."

He gestured to the empty tarmac. "And what good will that do you? Who will hear you? This is the executive terminal. The only people around are my people."

She reached up to capture her hair in one hand, keeping it from blowing in her face. "You don't understand. I can't go. I can't leave her."

"What are you talking about?"

"Jax." Her voice broke. "I've never been away from her before, not overnight. I can't leave her now."

"Jax?" he repeated impatiently. "What is that? Your cat?"

"No. My baby. My daughter."

"Your *daughter*?" he ground out.

She nodded, heart hammering. She felt sick to her stomach and so very scared. She'd forced herself to reach out to Rowan when she'd discovered she was pregnant, but he'd been even more hateful when she called him.

*"How did you get my number?"* he demanded.

*"Drakon."*

*"He shouldn't have given it to you."*

*"I told him it was important."*

*He laughed—a cold, scornful sound that cut all the way to her soul.*

*"Babe, in case you didn't get the message, it's over. I've nothing more for you. Now, pull yourself together and get on with your life."*

And so she had.

She didn't tell him about the baby. She didn't tell him he was having a daughter, and whatever qualms she had about keeping the information to herself were eventually erased by the memory of his coldness and hatefulness.

Her father had broken her heart, shaming her with his greed and selfishness, but Rowan was a close second. He was despicable. Like her father, the worst of the worst.

Thank goodness he wasn't in Jax's life. Logan couldn't even imagine the kind of father he'd be. Far better to raise Jax on her own than have Jax growing up with a father who couldn't, wouldn't, love her.

And now, facing Rowan on the tarmac, Logan knew she'd made the right decision. Rowan might be a military hero—deadly in battle, formidable in a combat zone—but he was insensitive to the point of abusive and she'd never allow him near her daughter.

"You're a *mother*?" he said.

She heard the bewildered note in his voice and liked it. She'd shocked him. Good. "Yes."

His brow furrowed. "Where is she now?"

"At home." Logan glanced at her watch. "Her sitter will leave at five. I need to be back by then."

"You won't be. You're not going back."

"And what about Jax? We'll just leave her in a crib until you decide you'll return me?"

His jaw worked, the small muscle near his ear pulling tight. "Drakon never mentioned a baby."

Her heart did a double beat and her stomach heaved. "They don't know."

"What?"

"No one knows."

"How can that be?"

"It might surprise you, but we don't do big family reunions anymore."

He folded his arms across his chest. "Who is her father?"

She laughed coolly. "I don't think that's any of your business, do you?"

He sighed. "What I meant is, can't her father take her while you're gone?"

"No."

"I think you need to ask—"

"No."

"Not a good relationship?"

She felt her lip curl. This would be funny if one enjoyed dark comedy. "An understatement if I ever heard one."

"Can her sitter keep her?"

"*No.*" The very idea of anyone *keeping* Jax made

Logan's heart constrict. "I've never been away from her for a night. She's a toddler…a baby…" Her voice faded and she dug her nails into her palms, waiting for Rowan to say something.

He didn't. He stared at her hard.

She couldn't read what he was thinking, but there was definitely something going on in that head, she could see it in his eyes, feel it in his tension. "I need to get home to her." Her voice sounded rough. She battled to maintain control. "Especially if there are paparazzi at the house. I don't want them doing anything—trying anything. I don't want her scared."

"Logan, I can't let you anywhere near the house. I'm sorry." He held up his hand when she started to protest. "I'll get her. But you must promise to stay here. No taking off. No running away. No frantic phone calls to anyone. Stay put on my plane and wait."

She glanced toward the white jet and spotted his staff waiting by the base of the stairs.

He followed her gaze. "My staff will make sure you're comfortable. As long as you stay here with them you won't be in any danger."

Stiffening, Logan turned back to face him. "Why would I be in danger? It's just the paparazzi."

"Bronson was shot late last night in London." Rowan's voice was clipped. "He's in ICU now, but the specialists believe he should make a full recovery—"

"Wait. What? Why didn't you say something earlier?" Bronson was the oldest of the five Copelands and the only son. "What happened?"

"Authorities are investigating now, but the prevailing theory is that Bronson was targeted because of your father. The deputy chief constable recommended that all members of your family be provided with additional security.

My team has already located Victoria and is taking her to a safe location. Your mother is with Jemma already. And now we have you."

Logan felt the blood drain from her head. Fear made her legs shake. "Please go get Jax. Hurry."

"Give me your phone."

"I won't call anyone—"

"That's not why I want your phone. I'm taking it so I can be you and make sure Joe understands what I need him to do."

"You're involving Joe?" she asked, handing him the phone.

"You trust him, don't you?"

She nodded. "The password is zero, three, three, one."

Rowan started for the helicopter and then turned around. "Didn't we meet March 31?"

She went hot all over. "That's not why it's my password." She heard her defensive tone and hated it.

"Never said it was. But it does make it easy for me to remember your code." And then he signaled the pilot to start up the chopper and the blades began whirling and he was climbing in and the helicopter was lifting off even before Rowan had shut the door.

# CHAPTER THREE

ROWAN WAS GONE for two hours and twenty-odd minutes, and during those long two plus hours, Logan couldn't let herself think about anything...

Not Bronson, who'd been hurt. Or her family who were all being guarded zealously to protect them from a nut job.

She couldn't think about her daughter or how frightened she must be.

She couldn't think about her huge event taking place tomorrow and how she now wouldn't be there to see it through.

She couldn't think about anything because once she started thinking, her imagination went wild and every scenario made her heartsick.

Every fear pummeled her, making her increasingly nauseous.

But of all her fears, Jax was the most consuming. She loved her brother and sisters but they were adults, and it sounded as if they now had a security team protecting them. But Jax...her baby...?

Logan exhaled slowly, struggling to keep it together. Rowan *had* to be successful. And there was no reason he wouldn't be. He was the world's leading expert in hostage and crisis situations and removing a toddler from a Santa Monica bungalow was not a crisis situation. But that didn't mean her heart didn't race and her stomach didn't heave and she didn't feel frantic, aware that all kinds of things could go wrong.

But Rowan being successful meant that he would be with Jax, and this terrified her. The haters and shamers had hardened her to the nonstop barbs and insults, but Jax was her weakness. Jax made her vulnerable. And maybe that's because Jax herself was so vulnerable.

A light from the cockpit drew her attention and she glanced up, noting the three men up front—two pilots and the male flight attendant.

They were an interesting-looking flight crew bearing very little resemblance to the pleasant, professional, middle-aged crew you'd find on a commercial plane. These three were lean, muscular and weathered. They looked so fit and so tan that it made her think they'd only recently retired from active duty with the military. As they spoke to each other in low voices, she tried to listen in, but it was impossible to eavesdrop from where she sat.

Abruptly the three men turned and looked at her and then the male flight attendant was heading her way.

"Did you need something, Miss Copeland?" he asked crisply. He didn't look American, but he didn't have an accent. He was an enigma, like the rest of the crew.

"Is there any water?"

"I'll bring you a bottle. Would you like a meal? Are you hungry?"

She shook her head. "I don't think I could eat. Just water."

But once she had the bottle of water, she just held it between her hands, too nervous to drink more than a mouthful.

The minutes dragged by, slowly turning into hours. She

wished someone would give her an update. She wished she knew *something*.

But just when she didn't think she could handle another minute of silence and worry, the distinctive sound of a helicopter could be heard.

She prayed it was Rowan returning—

The thought stopped her short. Just hours ago such a prayer would have struck her as ludicrous. But he'd gone after her baby and she was grateful for that.

Who would have ever thought she'd pray to see him again?

As the helicopter touched down the flight crew stood at the entrance of the jet as if prepared for battle.

Logan arched her brows. Rowan was serious about personal safety, wasn't he?

But then the helicopter was down and the door was opening. Rowan was the first to step out and he was holding Jax, and as he crossed the tarmac, Joe Lopez was close behind carrying two suitcases.

What was Joe doing? Had he insisted on accompanying Jax to be sure she was safe? Or had Rowan wanted Joe along in case Jax got scared?

Either way Logan was delighted when the men stepped onto the plane with the baby.

Jax squealed when she saw Logan. "Momma!"

Logan opened her arms and Rowan handed the child over. "Hello, sweet girl," Logan whispered, kissing her daughter's soft cheek again and again. "How's my baby girl?"

Jax turned her head to kiss Logan back. "I love Momma."

"And Momma loves you. What did you think of the helicopter?" Logan asked her, giving her a little squeeze. "Was it noisy?"

Jax nodded and clapped her hands to her head. "Don't like ear things. Bad."

Rowan met Logan's gaze over Jax's head. "Not a fan of the headset."

"Not surprised. She has a mind of her own," Logan said.

"She does like Joe, though. She insisted on sitting on his lap during the flight. He's good with her, too," Rowan said.

Logan glanced back toward the galley where the flight attendant was taking the two suitcases from her assistant. "It was nice of him to come. Or did you make him?"

"I didn't make Joe do anything. He is apparently very devoted to you—"

"Don't start again."

"Just saying, he's here because he insisted."

"I appreciate it. He's been awesome with her since the beginning." Logan frowned at the size of the two suitcases. "How long are we going to be gone?"

"Your buddy Joe did the packing. Apparently you girls need a lot when you travel."

Logan's eyes met Rowan's. She gave her head a slight shake, her expression mocking. "You sound a little jealous of him, you know."

"Me, *jealous*, of that...kid? Right." Rowan made a scornful sound and turned away as Joe approached Logan.

"You all right?" Joe asked Logan even as he handed Jax a sippy cup with water.

Logan nodded and shot Rowan's retreating back a disapproving look. "I hope he wasn't rude to you," she said to Joe. "If he was, don't take it personally. He's that way with everyone."

Joe smiled and shrugged. "I've met worse."

Logan gave him a look.

His smile broadened. "He doesn't bother me. And he was actually pretty sweet with Jax—"

"Don't say it. Don't want to hear it." Logan cut him short. "So is he going to send you back in the helicopter or are you having to grab a cab back? If you need a cab, just put it on my account. I won't have you paying for something like that. It'll be ridiculously expensive."

"I'll grab a rental car and drop it off at LAX." Joe hesitated a moment. "Are you going to be okay?"

Logan kissed the top of Jax's head and nodded. "Need tomorrow's event to go off without a hitch—"

"It will. The fund-raiser will be huge, and the fashion show will be wonderful. But you're the one I'm worried about."

"Don't. I'm fine. And my company…it's everything. It's my reputation. My livelihood. It's how I provide for Jax—" She broke off, overwhelmed by stress and the weight of her reality. Her reality was harsh. People didn't give her the same benefit of the doubt they gave others. She didn't get second chances or opportunities…no, she had to fight tooth and nail for every job, forced to prove herself over and over again.

"I'll handle it," Joe said quietly, his deep voice firm.

"Thank you."

And then he kissed Jax on the top of her head and he left.

Rowan didn't seem to even notice that Joe had gone and it burned Logan up, how arrogant and callous Rowan was. Joe had been a huge help and Rowan didn't thank him or care.

Why couldn't Logan fall for someone like Joe…someone smart and kind and caring? Someone with *emotions*?

And then as if able to read Logan's mind, Rowan was returning. "We need to go." He nodded at the toddler. "Are you going to hold her for takeoff, or do you want me to buckle her car seat into a chair next to you?"

"Which is safer?" Logan asked.

"Car seat," he answered promptly.

"Then let's do that."

"Has she ever been on a plane before?"

Logan shook her head. "We don't…go out…much." And seeing his expression she added, "We don't need the attention."

"Have things been that difficult?"

"You've no idea." And then she laughed because it was all she could do. The haters and shamers would not win. They wouldn't. She'd make sure of that, just as she'd make sure her daughter would grow up with a spine and become a woman with courage and strength.

Rowan glanced at his watch. They'd been flying four hours but still had a good four to five hours to go. He was glad that the toddler finally slept, though. Earlier she'd cried for nearly an hour when she couldn't have her blanket. Joe had brought the blanket when they met up at the Santa Monica airport. The blanket was either in a seat or on the floor of the helicopter or perhaps it got dropped on the tarmac during the transfer to the plane. Either way, the baby was inconsolable and Logan walked with Jax, up and down the short aisle, patting her little girl's back until Jax had finally cried herself to sleep on Logan's shoulder.

Now Logan herself was asleep in one of the leather chairs in a reclined position, the little girl still on her chest, the child's two miniature ponytails brushing Logan's chin.

Seeing Logan with the child made him uncomfortable.

He didn't like the ambivalence, either. He didn't like *any* ambivalence, preferring life tidy, organized, categorized into boxes that could be graded and stacked.

He'd put Logan into a box. He'd graded the box and labeled it, stacking it in the corner of his mind with other

bad and difficult memories. After he'd left her, after their
night together, he'd been troubled for weeks…months. It
had angered him that he couldn't forget her, angered him
that he didn't have more control over his emotions. He
shouldn't care about her. He shouldn't worry about her.
And yet he did.

He worried constantly.

He worried that someone, somewhere would hurt her.

He worried about her physical safety. He worried about
her emotional well-being. He'd been so hard on her. He'd
been ruthless, just the way he was with his men, and in his
world. But she wasn't a man, and she wasn't conditioned
to handle what he'd dished out.

He'd come so close, so many times to apologizing.

He'd come so close to saying he was wrong.

But he didn't. He feared opening a door that couldn't
be shut. There was no point bonding with a woman who
wasn't to be trusted. Trust was everything in his world,
and she'd lied to him once—Logan Lane, indeed—so why
wouldn't she lie again?

Maybe the trust issue would be less crucial if he had
a different job. Maybe if his work wasn't so sensitive he
could be less vigilant…but his work was sensitive, and
countless people depended on him to keep them safe, and
alive.

Just as Jax depended on her mother to keep her safe.

He wanted to hate Logan. Wanted to despise her. But
watching her sleep with Jax stirred his protective instinct.

At two years old, Jax was still more baby than girl, her
wispy blond hair a shade lighter than her mother's. They
both had long dark eyelashes and the same mouth, full and
pink with a rosebud for an upper lip.

Sleeping, Jax was a vision of innocence.

Sleeping, Logan was a picture of maternal devotion.

Together they made his chest ache.

Rowan didn't want his chest to ache. He didn't want to care in any way, but it was difficult to separate himself when he kept running numbers in his head.

March 31 plus forty weeks meant a December birthday. Jax had a December birthday. December 22 to be precise. He knew because Joe had located Jax's birth certificate at the house and put it in a file for Rowan. You couldn't just whisk a baby out of a country without any legal documentation. If they were flying on a commercial plane, he'd have to go through government channels, which would have required a passport.

But since they weren't flying on a private plane, his pilot had submitted a manifest—which had included Logan Copeland. The manifest had not included the baby as he hadn't known there was a baby until just hours ago.

The baby could potentially be an issue, but as Rowan had diplomatic immunity, he wasn't too worried for himself.

Logan was another matter. She could definitely find herself in hot water should various governments discover she'd smuggled a baby out of one country and into another.

Fortunately they would be landing on Rowan's private airstrip on his private property, so there shouldn't be guards or officers inspecting his jet, or interrogating his guests.

But if they did…what would he say about Jax?

The child born exactly forty weeks after March 31.

Aware that she was being studied, Logan opened her eyes. Rowan sat watching her in a leather chair opposite hers.

He wasn't smiling.

She just held his cool green gaze, her heart sinking. She didn't want to panic and yet there was something very quiet, and very thoughtful, in his expression and it made her imagine that he could see things he couldn't see and know things he couldn't possibly know.

He couldn't possibly know that Jax was his.

He couldn't possibly imagine that she would have slept only with him. Her one and only lover in twenty-seven years. That didn't happen anymore. Women didn't wait for true love…

And so she arched a brow, matching his cool expression, doing what she did best—*deflect, deflect, deflect*. "Was I snoring?"

"No."

"Was my mouth open, catching flies?"

"I want a DNA test."

The words were so quietly spoken that it took Logan a moment to process them. He wanted a DNA test. He did suspect…

*Deflect, deflect, deflect.* "That's awfully presumptuous, don't you think?"

"You said you were a virgin. You made a big fuss earlier about how I manhandled your hymen—"

"I did not say that."

"—which makes me doubt you were out getting laid by someone else in the following five to seven days."

"Your math is excellent. I commend you. Not just a skilled lover, but also a true statistician, except for the fact that Jax wasn't due for another month. She arrived early."

"Your sweet girl was almost nine pounds, my love. She wasn't early."

Logan's stomach heaved. He knew how much Jax weighed. He knew her birth date. What else did he know? "She's not yours," she repeated stubbornly.

"No, she hasn't been, but she should be, shouldn't she?"

Logan held her breath.

"We'll test tomorrow, after we land."

"You're not going to poke her with a needle—"

"We'll do a saliva swab. Painless."

*"Rowan."*

"Yes, Logan?"

Logan's heart was beating so fast she was afraid it'd wake Jax. "You don't even like children. You don't want them. And you despise girls—"

"Is this what you've been telling yourself the past three years? Is this your justification for keeping Jax from me?"

*You called me a whore. You said the worst, most despicable things to me.*

And yes, those words hurt, but that wasn't why she didn't tell him. "I tried," she said, her voice quiet but thankfully steady.

"And when was that?"

"When I called you. Remember that? I phoned to tell you, and instead of a 'How are you? Everything okay?' you demanded to know how I got your number." She stared Rowan down, her gaze unwavering. "Even when I told you that Drakon had given it to me because it was important, you were hateful. You mocked me, saying you'd given me all you could."

Her voice was no longer quiet and calm. It vibrated with emotion, coloring the air between them. "After you hung up, I cried myself sick, and then eventually I pulled myself together and was glad. *Glad* you wanted nothing to do me, glad you wanted nothing to do with us, glad that my daughter wouldn't have to grow up as I did, with a selfish, uncaring father."

For a long moment Rowan said nothing. He just studied her from his seat, his big, lean, powerful body relaxed, his expression thoughtful. He seemed as if he didn't have a care in the world, which put her on high alert. This was

Rowan at his most dangerous, and she suspected what made him so dangerous was that he cared.

He cared a great deal.

Finally he shifted and sighed. "There are so many things I could say."

Logan's heart raced and her stomach rolled and heaved. "Why don't you say them?"

"Because we are still hours away from Galway—"

"Galway?" she interrupted.

"—and I don't feel like arguing all the way to Ireland."

She blinked at him, taken aback. "We can't leave the US. I don't have a passport with me, and Jax doesn't even have one yet."

Rowan shrugged, unconcerned. "We're landing on a private airstrip. There won't be any customs or immigration officers on our arrival."

"And what about when we return? Don't you think it will be problematic then?"

"Could be. But Joe packed your passport when he packed for you, and he sent along Jax's birth certificate, so we do have that."

That's how Rowan knew Jax's birth date. That's how he knew what he knew. But how did Joe know where to find her legal documents? She'd never told him…

Logan watched the slow drumming of Rowan's fingers on his hard thigh, mesmerized by the bronze of his skin and the tantalizing movement of strong fingers, the drumming steady, rhythmic.

The man had good hands. They'd felt so good on her. His touch had a sensitivity and expertise that was so different from his reputation as an elite fighter…warrior…

He'd made her feel things she didn't think she could feel, but no more. Hope and beauty—

*No.* Couldn't go there again, couldn't remember, couldn't

let herself fantasize that what had been was anything but sex. He'd made it clear she was just a lay. Sweat and release…exercise.

Her eyes burned and she swallowed hard, disgusted with herself for still letting his callous words upset her, hurt her. She shouldn't care. She shouldn't.

And yet she did.

Maybe if the sex hadn't been so good she could play this game. Maybe if she hadn't felt hope and joy, and maybe if he hadn't made her feel beautiful… Things she hadn't felt in so long. So many people had been hateful about her father. The world had become ugly and hostile, and then Rowan had been the opposite. He'd been light and heat and emotion and she couldn't help feeling connected to him. Bonded.

And then he discovered the Copeland part of her name, having missed that the night before…

Logan exhaled slowly, head light and spinning, dizzy from holding her breath too long. "I can't do this with you," she said lowly, her hand reaching up to adjust Jax on her chest. "Not with her here."

"What do you think we're going to do?"

"Fight. Be hateful." Her voice sounded strained to her own ears. "But Jax shouldn't be part of that. It's not fair to her, or good for her—"

"I've no desire to hurt my daughter," he interrupted. "And I don't need a damn DNA test to confirm it. We'll have it done so we can correct her birth certificate, but I don't need it to prove anything. She's obviously mine."

"Ours," she whispered, and it killed her to do it, killed her to say it but Jax had to be protected, no matter the cost. "Obviously ours."

The corner of Rowan's mouth lifted and his expression turned rueful. "I suppose it's a good thing that your father died. In time we will even view his passing as a blessing because it brought us all together. You, me and our daughter."

There was nothing frightening in his tone. If anything he sounded…amused. But Rowan's sense of humor was nothing like hers, and her heart lurched.

"So what is the next step?" he asked, smiling faintly, green eyes gleaming. "A wedding at the castle? And do we do it before or after your father's funeral?"

Thank God she was sitting. Thank God for armrests. Thank God Jax stirred then and let out a whimper, saving Logan from having to answer.

Jax whimpered once more and stretched, flinging out small arms in an attempt to get more comfortable.

Logan wanted to whimper, too.

This was crazy, so crazy.

Rowan was crazy.

"I think we do it before," he added reflectively. "It will give everyone something to celebrate. Yes, there will be sadness over your father's life being cut short—he was such a good man, so devoted to his family and community—but then everyone will be able to rejoice over our happy and surprising news. We're not just newlyweds, but proud parents of a two-year-old girl."

"You hate my father, and you hate me—"

"That's the past," he said gently, cutting her short. "It's time to leave the past in the past and concentrate on the future. And you're going to be my wife and we'll have more children—"

"You're having a really good time with this, aren't you?"

His broad shoulders shifted. "I'm trying to be positive, yes."

"I don't think you're trying to be positive as much as sadistic," she retorted, fighting panic because she didn't think Rowan was teasing. He seemed quite serious, which was terrifying as Rowan's entire career was based on his ability to play dirty. "We're not marrying. There won't be more children. There is no relationship. There has never been a relationship. So don't start throwing your weight around because I won't put up with it."

He had the audacity to laugh. "No? What will you do? Call Joe?"

Her cheeks burned. "You have such a problem with him. If I didn't know you better, I'd say you were jealous."

"I don't even know where to begin with that statement… so many ways I could run with it." He smiled at her, a charming smile that made her want to leap from her chair and run.

"Joe," he said politely, "works for *me*."

When her lips parted he held up a hand to stop her.

"He's worked for me since the day you hired him. He didn't attend USC. He never studied art, communications or design. And he's not twenty-four. He's thirty-one, and before he came to work for Dunamas, he was a member of Delta Force."

Logan couldn't wrap her head around what Rowan was telling her. Joe was not a military guy. Joe was young and sweet and hardworking…

But Rowan misunderstood her baffled expression. "First Special Forces Operational Detachment Delta," he said.

"I don't need an explanation for the abbreviation Delta Force. I need to understand how someone I hired from a pool of candidates worked for you."

"They all worked for me."

"No."

"How many résumés and cover letters did you get?"

"Six. No, five. One withdrew hers."

"How many did you interview?"

"Four."

"How many in person?"

"The top three."

"Trish Stevens, Jimmy Gagnier and Joe Lopez. Trish wanted too much money. Jimmy made you uncomfortable because he knew about your family. And Joe was just so dang grateful to have a job." The corner of his mouth quirked but he wasn't smiling. "And you believed him because you wanted—needed—to believe him."

"But I called his references…" Her voice faded as she heard herself and realized how foolish she sounded. She stared hard at a point just past Rowan's shoulder, willing her eyes to stop stinging, willing the awful lump in her throat to stop aching.

She'd trusted Joe.

She'd trusted him with her work and her family and her life…

"I thought he was a good person," she whispered, feeling impossibly betrayed.

"He is. He would have died for you. No questions asked."

"I'm sure that must have cost you a pretty penny."

"Joe did protect you," Rowan said. "And he wasn't a spy—"

"I don't believe that for a minute."

"If he was a spy, he would have told me about the baby. He never did." Rowan's voice deepened, hardened. "His job was to protect you, and he did. He was so devoted to you that he also protected you, and Jax, from me."

Logan had nothing to say to that. She stared at Rowan, stunned, because theoretically, if Joe was employed by Rowan, he probably should have told Rowan he was protecting a woman and a baby…

"Yes," Rowan said. "He took his job as your security

detail very, very seriously. He never once mentioned anything about a pregnancy or a baby or that he spent lots of time working from your home."

She almost laughed, feeling slightly hysterical. "Do you have any idea the things I had him do? The errands after work? The trips to the dry cleaner? He even helped feed Jax dinners when I was working away at my computer…" Logan swallowed hard. "I thought he loved her. And maybe it wasn't love, but I thought he really did care about us."

For several minutes there was just silence and then Rowan made a low, rough sound. "He did," Rowan said shortly. "For two years Joe protected you and your secret. He shouldn't have, though. That was a critical error on his part. I've fired him. He'll find it difficult getting another high-level security job." And then Rowan walked away, heading to the galley.

Logan watched his back, the sting of tears prickling her eyes. She didn't think it was possible, but her very bad day had just gotten worse.

# CHAPTER FOUR

ROWAN WAS POURING HIMSELF a neat shot of whiskey when Logan appeared in the narrow kitchen galley.

She stood in the doorway, arms crossed over her chest. She was so much thinner than she'd been three years ago. He'd known she worked hard, but he hadn't expected her to look quite so stressed. If he'd known she was pregnant… if he'd known there was a child…

He threw back the shot and looked at her. "Yes, love?"

"I'm not your love."

His fingers itched to pour another drink but he never had more than one. At least, never more than one in a twelve-hour span. He couldn't afford to lose his head. Ever.

But he had lost it once. He'd lost it March 31 three years ago to *her.* The evidence of that was curled up in a chair, hair in two tiny ponytails. They'd used protection the night of the bachelor auction. He knew he'd used protection. Clearly it hadn't been the right protection, or enough.

"Have you heard anything about Bronson? Is he stable or still in critical condition?"

"Bronson will remain in ICU for another few days, but he's been stabilized. The decision to keep him in ICU is for his protection. It's easier to secure the ICU unit than another floor."

"And Victoria? Where is she is right now? Who exactly has her?"

"By now your sister should be with Drakon and Morgan—"

"Oh, that's going to go over beautifully."

"Why?"

"They don't get along. At all."

"Drakon and Victoria?"

"Morgan and Victoria." She frowned. "I wouldn't leave Victoria there. She should go to Jemma. They're close. Victoria will be far happier there."

"It's too late for that. What's done is done and hopefully your sisters will realize that this isn't the time to bicker."

Her eyebrows rose. "They don't bicker. They've had a massive falling out, over my father. It's painful for everyone."

"Then I wish Drakon well because it's his problem now." Rowan leaned back against the narrow galley counter, the stainless steel cool against his back. He allowed his gaze to slide over Logan's slender frame, studying her intently. "Why didn't you get an abortion?"

If his question shocked her, she gave no indication. "It wasn't the right choice for me," she answered, her voice firm and clear.

She was good, he thought. She sounded so grounded and smart and reasonable, which just provoked him even more.

He gripped the counter's edge tightly. It was that or grab her by the shoulder and drag her into his arms. His kiss wouldn't be kind.

He was not feeling kind.

It was difficult to feel kind when his cock throbbed in his trousers and his body felt hard and hungry.

He remembered the smell of her and the taste of her

and how soft and warm and wet she'd been as he'd kissed her there, between her legs, and made her body tighten and break with pleasure. And then he'd thrust in, burying himself hard, and she'd groaned and stiffened and he'd thought that had been pleasure, too.

Now he knew he'd taken her virginity ruthlessly. Not knowing…

Not knowing the first damn thing about her.

A Copeland. A virgin. A society princess dethroned.

"Don't fire Joe," she said, breaking the tense silence. Her voice was husky. He heard the pleading note, and it made him even angrier. Why did it bother him that she was pleading for Joe? Was it because he worried that she cared for him? Or was it because he wanted her to plead for him…

She'd begged him three years ago, begged for his hands and his mouth, begged to be touched and taken, and he'd obliged.

Now look at them. Parents of a tiny girl.

He wouldn't ignore his responsibilities. He wouldn't punish the girl the way he'd been punished when his father knocked his mother up.

His father who drank too much and let his fists fly. His mother who drank too much and forgot to come home.

Not that he blamed her. Home was not a nice place to be.

"Please," Logan started again. "Please don't—"

"Joe doesn't need you begging for his job," Rowan said curtly, unable to bear hearing her plead any longer. It was far too reminiscent of a childhood he hated. It was far too reminiscent of a person he didn't want to be. "He knew what he was doing. He made his own choices—"

"For Jax."

"For you," he corrected. "I know he cared for you. I

know he developed…feelings…for you. I know when his attachment became more than just a strong sense of duty."

"And yet you left him on the job."

Rowan really wanted another drink, craving the burn and the heat in his veins because maybe then he wouldn't want to push her up against the galley wall and put his hands into her hair and take her soft mouth and make her whimper for him.

He felt like an animal.

He didn't want to be an animal.

His work usually kept him focused but right now he had none. Just her and her wide, searching blue eyes and that dark pink mouth that demanded to be kissed.

"No," he ground out, knuckles tight as he gripped the stainless counter harder. "I didn't *leave* him on the job. I relieved him months ago. Back before the Christmas holidays. He refused to step down. He refused to abandon you."

Her lips curved, tremulous. "Unlike you?"

If she'd been icy and mocking he could have ignored the jab. If she'd shown her veneer, he would have let her be. But her unsteady words coupled with the tremble of her lip made his chest squeeze, the air bottled within.

He'd hurt her, because he'd meant to hurt her.

He was very good at what he did.

Rowan reached for her wrist, his fingers circling her slender bones and he pulled her toward him. She stiffened but didn't fight him. If anything she'd gone very still.

"Let me see your head," he said gruffly, bringing her hips almost to his. He lifted a heavy wave of honey-colored hair from her forehead to inspect her temple.

With one hand still in her hair, he tipped her head, tilting this way and that to get a proper look. It didn't look too bad. She must have cleaned the wound while he'd gone to pick up Jax. The cut was scabbing, and he saw the start of a dark bruise. The bruise would be uglier tomorrow, but all in all, she was healing.

"I'm sorry I didn't catch you," he said, his deep voice still rough. They might not be on good terms but he didn't like that all he did was bring her pain. "You went down hard."

"I've survived far worse," she answered, her smile full of bravado, but the bold smile didn't reach her blue eyes, and in those blue eyes fringed by thick black lashes there was a world of hurt and shadows. Far too many shadows.

He tipped her head farther back to look into her eyes, trying to see where she'd been and all that had happened in the past three years and then he felt a stab of regret, and blame.

He'd left her out there, hanging.

He'd left her, just as she'd said.

He, who protected strangers, hadn't protected *her*.

His head dropped, his mouth covering hers. It was a kiss to comfort her, a kiss to apologize for being such an ass, and yet the moment his mouth touched hers he forgot everything but how warm she was and how good she felt against him. Her mouth was so very soft and warm, too, and her chest rose and fell with her quick gasp, the swell of her breasts pressing against his chest.

He had not been celibate for the past three years. He liked women and enjoyed sex, and he'd found pleasure with a number of women but Logan didn't feel like just any woman—she was different. She felt like his. But he didn't want to explore that thought, not when he wanted to explore her, and he slid a hand down the length of her back, soothing her even as he coaxed her closer, heat in his veins, hunger making him hard.

He wasn't going to force her, though. She could push

him away at any moment. He'd let her go the moment she said no, the moment she put a hand to his chest and pressed him back.

And then her hand moved to his chest, and her fingers grabbed at his shirt, and she tugged on the shirt, tugging him toward her.

The heat in his veins became a fire.

He deepened the kiss, his tongue tracing the seam of her lips until she opened her mouth. His tongue flicked over her lower lip and then found the tip of hers and teased that, and then the inside of her upper lip, teasing the delicate swollen skin until he felt her nails dig into his chest, her slender frame shuddering. He captured her hip, holding her close, wanting nothing more than to bury himself in her and make her cry his name again…

She wasn't like any other woman. He'd never met another woman he wanted this much.

The kiss became electric, so hot he felt as if he was going to explode. He didn't want to want her like this. He didn't want to want anyone like this. He didn't want his control tested, didn't want to feel as if he couldn't get enough, that he'd never have enough, that what he missed, needed, wanted was right here in this woman—

He broke off the kiss and stepped back. He was breathing hard, his shaft throbbing but that was nothing compared to what was happening in his chest, within his heart.

She was not the right one for him.

She couldn't be.

He didn't like spoiled, entitled society girls, and he didn't respect women who'd never had to work for anything…

"One of us should be with Jax," he said curtly. "Make sure she's safe in case there's turbulence."

"I was just on my way back to her," Logan replied turning around and walking away, but not before he saw the flush in her cheeks and the ripe plumpness of her pink lips.

He nearly grabbed her again, wanting to finish what he'd started.

Instead he let her go, body aching, mind conflicted.

There was no love lost between them. They couldn't even carry on a civil conversation but that didn't matter if he took her to bed. They didn't have to like each other. In fact, it might even be better if they didn't like each other. It didn't matter with them. The sex would still be hot.

Logan returned to her seat and carefully scooped Jax back into her arms and sat down with her daughter, not because Jax needed to be held but because Logan needed Jax for safety. Security.

Rowan's kiss had shaken her to the core.

Her heart still pounded, her body flooded with wants and needs that could destroy her. Rowan was not good for her. Rowan was danger…

She swallowed hard and closed her eyes, determined to clamp down on her emotions, determined to slow her pulse.

She didn't want him. She couldn't want him. She couldn't forget what happened last time, and she wasn't even talking about the blisteringly hot sex, but the emptiness afterward. The sex hadn't just been sex. It hadn't felt like sweat and exercise…release…it'd felt transformative.

It'd been…bliss.

And then he'd walked out of her Santa Monica house, door slamming behind him, and her heart had shattered into a thousand pieces. Never mind what he'd done to her self-respect.

She couldn't be turned on now. She couldn't be so stupid as to imagine that he'd be different, that the lovemaking would be safer or that the aftermath would be less destructive.

He was fire. And when he touched her, she blistered and living with burns wasn't her idea of a calm, centered, happy life.

She needed a calm, centered, happy life. It was the only way to provide for Jax. The only way to raise Jax in a healthy home.

Rowan Argyros might be seduction on two legs, but he wasn't the daddy she wanted for Jax, or the partner she needed—and then suddenly he was back, dropping into the leather seat across from hers and extending his legs, his dark head tipping back, his eyes closing, hiding his intense green eyes.

But even with his eyes closed the air felt charged. Magnetic.

She glared at him, hating how her pulse jumped and raced and her body grew hot all over again just because he was close.

Without even opening his eyes he said, "We still have a good four plus hours to go. I'd sleep if I were you. You'll feel better—"

"This is not my first international trip," she said curtly, cutting him off. Of course he'd think she was staring at him. And yes, she was, but that was beside the point.

The edge of his mouth lifted. "Suit yourself."

"Yes, I will."

The corner lifted higher.

Her stomach tightened. Her pulse raced. She pressed her lips into a thin, hard line, trying to hold back all the angry words she wanted to hurl at him.

He brought out the worst in her. He did. She needed to get away from him, and the sooner the better. But how?

She wasn't dealing with an ordinary man. If she set

aside her personal feelings for a moment, she'd admit that
he was extraordinary in every way, but that was the problem. With Rowan she couldn't set aside her personal feelings. With Rowan it was nothing but personal.

The night he'd spent with her had changed her forever.
His touch was so profound that he might as well have taken
a hammer and chisel to her heart, carving his name into
the very marrow of her being.

Even now she could feel him as if his hand was on hers.

As if his chest was pressed to hers.

She could feel him because just the smell, touch, taste
of him made her burn. She wanted him still. She wanted
more.

But more would break her. More would crack her all
the way open, draining her until there was nothing left of
Logan Copeland.

But maybe that's what he wanted. Maybe he wanted
to destroy her.

If so, he was off to a good start.

Logan woke to the sound of murmured voices. Opening her
eyes she spotted Rowan standing across the aisle with Jax
in his arms. They were facing a big screen and watching
a Disney movie featuring fish, and Rowan was discussing the cartoon with her. Jax had her finger in her mouth
and seemed more fascinated by Rowan than the huge blue
tang searching for her parents.

Jax was already a petite little girl and tucked against
Rowan's chest, in his muscular arms, she looked impossibly small.

Logan swallowed around the lump filling her throat.
Jax was her world. Her center. Her sunshine. And Logan
didn't want to share her, and she most definitely didn't
want to share her with someone who didn't deserve her.

Just like that, she heard another voice in her head.

It was her mother's voice, raised, emotional. *He doesn't deserve us...he doesn't deserve any of us...*

She must have shifted, or maybe she made a sound, because suddenly Rowan was turning and looking at her. "You were out," he said.

"How long?"

"Long enough for us to watch a movie." And right on cue the film's credits rolled.

"Dory," Jax said to Logan, pointing to the enormous flat screen.

Logan smiled at her daughter. "You love Dory, don't you?"

Jax nodded and, popping her finger back into her mouth, looked at Rowan. "Dory can't 'member."

Rowan nodded. "But she still found a way to be successful. That's what's important. Never give up." And then his gaze met Logan's over Jax's head. "A good lesson for all of us, I think."

Logan left her seat and reached for her daughter. "I'll take her. See if we can find a snack—"

"She ate while you were sleeping," he answered, handing her back. "She likes chicken. And she couldn't get enough cantaloupe."

And then he was walking away, and Logan gave Jax a little cuddle and kiss, even as her heart pounded, aware that everything in her life had changed. There were men you could escape. There were men you could forget. But Rowan Argyros was neither.

They landed just before noon on a long, narrow runway that sliced an emerald green field in two. The touchdown was so smooth it felt like they'd landed on glass. Logan kissed the top of Jax's head. Her daughter had been awake for the past several hours and she was relaxed and content at the moment, quietly sucking on her thumb. Logan had worked hard to discourage the habit but she let it go now as it probably helped Jax's ears adjust to the change in pressure.

The jet slowed steadily and then did a smooth turn on the landing strip, and began a long taxi back the way they'd just come.

Logan returned her attention to the emerald expanse beyond. It was misty outside, the windows covered with fine water droplets. Now that they were on the ground she could see that the fields were actually a vast lawn, and the green lawns gradually rolled up to a hill dominated by a large gray castle with a tall square stone tower and smaller towers at different corners.

As they taxied, they headed closer to the castle, and different features came into view. The big square tower's parapet. The tall Gothic windows. The arches above the narrow windows. There were no trees or shrubs to soften the starkness of the castle. Instead it just rose up from a sea of green, and it didn't strike Logan as a particularly friendly castle. Maybe it was the dark sky and drizzly rain, but the forbidding exterior made her think it was a fortress, not a home, and the last thing she wanted was to be locked up. Trapped.

"Who lives there?" she asked uneasily, hoping against hope that this was not the Irish estate Morgan had talked about. Morgan and Drakon had visited Rowan's Irish estate a year or so ago and she'd made it sound palatial. This was not palatial.

"I do." Rowan shifted in his chair, legs extended, hands folded on his lean flat stomach. "When here."

She glanced out the rain-splattered window and sucked on the inside of her lip, trying to maintain her calm because as impressive as the castle was, it lacked warmth. She couldn't find anything inviting about such a massive building. "I can see why you don't spend that much time in Ireland."

"I'm here quite often, and I am very fond of the place. I gather you don't like it?"

"It's stark." She hesitated, before adding, "And very gray."

"There's a lot of stone," he agreed. "But it's sturdy. The oldest towers are over six hundred years old. The newer sections are two hundred years. But when I bought it, I refurbished the interior and you'll find it quite comfortable." His smile was crooked. "I love my mother's country but I must have a little too much of my father's Greek blood, or maybe I'm just getting older, but I don't like being cold."

Her gaze met his and there was something mocking in his eyes, but it wasn't unkind as much as challenging. He seemed to be daring her to say something, daring her to disagree, but looking at him there was nothing old or weak about him. He was powerful from the top of his head to the intense gold of his eyes, to the tips of his toes.

"I somehow don't think the cold bothers you all that much," she answered. "At least, I remember your saying three years ago that you trunk it when you surf in California. Even in winter."

He shrugged carelessly and yet there was a flicker of heat in his eyes, as if surprised that she'd remembered. But of course she remembered. That was the problem. She remembered *everything*.

"I don't like wetsuits." Rowan's deep voice rumbled in his chest and his head was turned, his gaze fixed on the drizzly landscape beyond the window. "Not even here, when I'm surfing in Wales or Scotland."

The jet had rolled to a stop. The flight attendant was at

the door. Logan glanced at him and then at Rowan who'd also unfastened his seat belt and was rising.

"Are there good waves in the UK?" she asked.

"One of my favorite breaks is in Scotland. Thurso East. I like Fresh in Pembrokeshire, too." He gazed down at her for a moment, a faint smile playing at his lips and yet the smile didn't touch his eyes. Those were a cool green, a much cooler green than the emerald lawns outside, and then he extended a hand to her. "Fresh can be dangerous, though. The reef break is heavy and significant, and then there is the army firing range above. It's not for beginners."

"And you like that it's frightening."

"I'd call it exhilarating." His lips curved ever so slightly, his expression almost mocking. "Just as I am finding you exhilarating. I had no idea I had a family. Everything is changing. *Fáilte abhaile*," he said in Gaelic. "Welcome home."

She'd had three plus years to get over him. Three years to grow a thick skin...an armor...and yet he'd dismantled her defenses with just a few words, a careless smile, a hot, searing kiss...

Logan held her own cool smile, even as she drew a slow breath to hide the frantic beating of her heart. "It shall be fascinating to see your home," she said, unbuckling her seat belt and rising, shifting Jax to her hip. "I consider it an adventure. I have always enjoyed a good adventure. And then it will be time for me to return home. As fun as it is to have a little getaway, I've a business in Los Angeles, and obligations there—"

"Your obligations are to your family first, and as the mother of my child, you and I will want to make the necessary adjustments to ensure that you and she are safe." His gaze never wavered. "Castle Ros is safe. If you do not wish to live here year-round we can discuss other options, but there is no place in the United States where you'd be safe right now."

"I don't wish to argue in front of Jax—"

"Then let's not."

She ground her teeth together, determined to keep her composure as an emotional outburst would only alienate Rowan and frighten her daughter. "You don't want me," she said softly, urgently. "And I don't want you—"

"You wanted me very much three years ago. You'll want me again."

Her gaze swiftly dropped to her daughter. Her voice dropped even lower. "Everything I cherished was stripped away by my father. Love is all I have left, and you are not going to take that from me. I deserve the chance to be loved, and we both know that is not something you're offering. And love is the only reason I'd ever marry. The only one," she repeated.

And then, desperate for air and space, she walked past him and headed for the plane door, too agitated to return for her purse and Jax's diaper bag. Purses and diaper bags could be retrieved…replaced. Her sanity was another matter.

Rowan followed Logan off the jet and took a seat next to her in the armored car. He was sure she didn't know the luxury sedan had bulletproof glass and extra paneling in the sides. She didn't need to know that. She didn't need to know that the perimeter of his estate was walled and patrolled and every security measure had been taken to make Castle Ros one of the safest places in Europe— whether for a head of state needing protection or his own woman and daughter.

His gaze rested on Logan's profile.

His woman.

She was.

She'd been his from the moment he laid eyes on her at the auction. She hadn't even known that he'd seen her long before she'd noticed him. He'd picked her from the others, chosen her from every woman there as the one he'd wanted, and he'd willed it, made it happen, focusing on her so that she couldn't help but know who he was…couldn't help but feel his interest and desire.

She, who was working that night at the auction, had scrambled to bid, and he'd kept his attention locked on her throughout the bidding, and she'd done what he'd demanded…

She'd won him.

And he'd rewarded her. All night long.

And as the night turned to morning, he'd lain in bed next to her, watching her sleep and listening to her breathe, and wondering how to keep her and incorporate her into a life where he was rarely in one place long.

He was a bachelor. He needed to be a bachelor. And yet with her he felt settled, committed. He felt as if he'd come home, which was impossible as he'd never had a true home. He'd never belonged anywhere—he'd shifted between continents and countries, languages and cultures. Rowan had been raised as a nomad and outsider, caught between his fierce, moody, ambitious Greek father and his kind but unstable Irish mother. After the initial love-lust wore off, his parents couldn't get along. He still remembered the arguing when he was very young. They fought because there was never enough money, and never enough success. His father was full of schemes and plans, always looking for that one big break that would make him rich, while his mother just wanted peace. She didn't need a big windfall, she just wanted his father home. And then his father hit the jackpot, or so he thought, until he was arrested and sent to prison for white-collar crime.

The time away broke the family.

It broke what was left of the marriage and his mother.

Or maybe what broke the marriage, and his mother, was losing Devlin, Rowan's little brother. Devlin drowned while Father was in prison.

Rowan tensed, remembering. Devlin's death at two and three quarters had been the beginning of the end.

Rowan's father blamed Rowan's mother. Rowan's mother blamed Rowan's father. And then Rowan's father was out of jail, and the fighting just started over again. Rowan was glad to be sent to boarding school in England, and he told himself he was glad when his parents finally separated, because maybe, finally, the fighting would end. But the divorce dragged on for years, and school holidays became increasingly chaotic and painful. Sometimes he'd visit one parent in one country, while other times neither parent wanted him and if there was no classmate to invite him home, he'd remain at school, which was in many ways preferable to visits with strangers, including his parents who became little more than strangers as the years went by.

After finishing school, he went to university in America, and then returned to Britain to serve in the Royal Navy and never again returned home. Because there was no home. He'd never felt at home, which is why the attachment to Logan had been unsettling.

How could she feel like home when he didn't know what home was? How could he care for her when he didn't know her?

It had been almost a relief to discover she was a Copeland. She had been too good to be true. His rage had been swift and focused, and he'd let her feel the full impact of his disappointment. But it wasn't Logan he was truly angry with. He was angry with himself for dropping his guard and allowing himself to feel. Emotions were dangerous. Emotions were destructive. He couldn't let himself make that mistake again.

And now she was back in his life, and she wasn't merely a beautiful but problematic woman, she was also the mother of his child.

And that changed everything. That changed him. It had to change him. There was no way he'd allow his child to be caught between two adults battling for control. Nor would he let Logan disappear with his daughter the way his mother, Maire, had disappeared with him after Devlin's death.

So there would be a wedding, yes, but beyond that?

Rowan didn't have all the answers yet. He wasn't sure how he'd keep Logan and Jax in Ireland. He wasn't sure how he'd ensure that they couldn't disappear from his life. He only knew that it couldn't happen. And it wouldn't happen. He'd keep Logan close, he'd make her want to stay, and if he couldn't do it through love, he'd do it through touch…sex. Love wasn't the only way to bond with a woman. Touch and pleasure would melt her, weaken her, creating bonds that would be difficult, if not impossible, to break.

Was it fair? No. But life wasn't fair. Life was about survival, and Rowan was an expert survivalist.

*Fáilte abhaile mo bride*, he repeated silently, glancing once more at Logan's elegant profile, appreciating anew her stunning gold-and-honey beauty. *Welcome home, my bride.*

# CHAPTER FIVE

THE LUXURIOUS INTERIOR of Castle Ros hid its technology well. At first glance one didn't see the modern amenities, just the sumptuous appointments. The scattered rugs and plush carpets. The rich paneling and decoratively papered walls. The glow of lights in intricate fixtures. The oil portraits and massive landscapes in ornate gold frames. But then as Logan settled into her suite of rooms, a suite that adjoined Rowan's, she noticed the electrical outlets and USB ports tucked into every surface and corner.

There was a remote on the bedside table that controlled the temperature, and the blackout blinds at the windows, and an enormous painting over the fireplace that turned into a flat-screen TV. A refrigerator, sink and marble-topped counter had been tucked into one of the adjoining closets. On the white marble counter stood an espresso machine, and next to that was a lacquered box lined with pods of coffee. Milks and snacks filled the refrigerator. A small wine rack was stocked with bottles of red and white wine.

Apparently Rowan—or his estate manager—had thought of everything. There was no reason Logan couldn't be comfortable in the lavish suite.

Now Jax was another matter.

The castle wasn't child-friendly. There wasn't a small bed or even a chair suitable for a two-year-old anywhere, never mind the massive fireplaces—with fires—missing screens, and the steep stone staircases without a gate or barrier to slow a curious toddler's exploration.

But before Logan could voice her concerns, Rowan was already aware of the problem. "I recognize that the house poses a danger for Jax. While it's impossible to make the entire castle child-safe, I can certainly ensure that she has rooms—or an entire floor—that have been made secure, free of hazards, giving her plenty of space to play and move about."

And then he was gone, and Logan was alone with Jax in her huge suite with the high ceilings, crackling fire and tall, narrow windows.

Logan frowned at the fire. At least this one had a grate and screen, but the fire worried her.

But then, everything worried her. She'd lost control. Her carefully constructed world was in pieces, shattered by the appearance of Rowan Argyros.

He wasn't supposed to be in her life. She didn't want him in her life. She didn't want him near Jax. And yet here they all were, locked down in his high-tech, high-security castle.

She needed to get away. She needed to get Jax away from here as soon as possible. Logan didn't know how. She just knew it had to be done, and quickly. And while time was of the essence, strategy would be important as it wasn't going to be easy leaving Rowan's fortified home, nor would it be simple sneaking a two-year-old away.

After a bath and a light meal, Logan and Jax napped and then before Logan was ready to be awake, Jax was up and eager to play.

Logan's head throbbed. She needed sleep. Her body seemed to think it was the middle of the night—and back in California it was—but Jax was adjusting to the time change far better and Logan allowed the busy toddler to take all the shimmering silk pillows to the huge empty walk-in closet to play.

Logan made coffee and sat down with a notebook to figure out the next steps to take, and she was still sitting with the notebook—pages perfectly blank—when a knock sounded at the door.

Opening the bedroom door, she discovered a fresh-faced young woman in the hall.

"I'm Orla." The young woman introduced herself with a firm handshake and quick smile. "I've been a nanny for five years, but I'm not just a child minder, I'm a certified teacher, specializing in early education. So where is my lovely girl? I'm looking forward to meeting her."

Logan drew a short, rough breath, as Orla stepped past, entering the bedroom suite. "I'm sorry," she said awkwardly. "There must be a mistake. I haven't hired anyone."

"Your husband—"

"I don't have a husband."

Orla turned around and faced Logan. "Mr. Argyros—"

"Not my husband."

"Your fiancé—"

"He's not my fiancé."

The young woman didn't blink or flush or stammer. Her steady blue gaze met Logan's and held. "Your daughter's father."

Logan bit down on her tongue. She had no reply for that.

"He hired my services," Orla continued in the same calm, unflappable tone, her dark hair drawn back in a sleek, professional ponytail. Orla appeared to be a good five to ten years younger than Logan, and yet she was managing to making Logan feel as if she was a difficult child. "He said there'd been a recent death in the family," she added, "and you had matters to attend to. I'm here to help make everything easier for you."

Again, Logan couldn't think of an appropriate response. Somehow Rowan was getting the best of her, and he wasn't even here. "But I'm not working. I don't need any *help* with my daughter." She tensed as she heard her voice rise. She was sounding plaintive and that wouldn't do. "I enjoy my daughter's company very much, and right now I need her. She's such a comfort."

"But the wedding preparations will only tire her out. I can promise you she'll have great fun with me. I've brought toys and games and dolls. Does Jax like playing with dolls? I have a set of little fairies—they're a family and absolutely adorable—and most girls—"

"Fairies?" The connecting door to the massive walk-in closet flew open and Jax came running out, dragging one of the embroidered silk pillows behind her. She'd been happy in the closet, but apparently playing with fairies was far more appealing than tasseled silk pillows. "I love fairies!"

Orla was already on one knee, putting herself at eye level with Jax. "I have a whole family of fairies in my bag. Would you like to see?"

Jax nodded vigorously, and Logan held her breath, counted to five, and then ten, aware that her immediate presence was not needed here. "If you don't mind, I'll go have a word with Rowan."

Jax ignored her and Orla just flashed a cheerful smile. "Of course, Ms. Copeland. We'll be here, having a healthy snack and creating our fairy garden. We'll show you our garden when you're back."

Rowan wasn't surprised to see Logan at the door of his office. He rolled back from his desk where he'd been reading updates on situations he was monitoring and answering brief emails with even briefer replies.

He casually propped one foot on top of the other as she entered. "Everything all right?"

"No," she said curtly, crossing the floor. She'd changed since they'd arrived, and was dressed now in black trousers and a black knit sweater that clung to her high full breasts and hugged her narrow waist. Her thick, honey hair was parted in the middle, and the long, straight silk strands framed her face, drawing attention to the arched brows and haunting blue of her eyes.

He'd remembered she was pretty, but had forgotten how her beauty was such a physical thing. She crackled with energy, and just looking at her made his blood heat. "What's happened?" he asked, tamping down the desire. "Maybe I can help."

"You're the problem, and you know it." She stood before him, a hand on one hip, drawing attention to her lean figure, made even longer by her black leather boots. The heels on her leather boots were high. And incredibly sexy.

"Me?" he drawled.

Her arched eyebrow lifted higher, her expression incredulous, and Rowan didn't think she'd ever looked so fierce, or so desirable.

The fierceness was new, as was the crackling energy. She hadn't been fierce three years ago. She hadn't burned with this intensity, either. Becoming a mother had changed her.

He liked it. He liked her on fire. But then, he'd always loved a good fight, and she was itching for a fight now.

"Would you like to sit down?" He gestured to a chair not far from the desk. "We can talk—"

"You're not my partner or spouse," she said, cutting him short. "You will never be my partner or spouse, and you've no right to hire a nanny for my daughter without my permission." Temper flashed in her eyes. "Are you listening, Rowan? You need to understand what I'm saying."

His upper lip ached to curl. He wanted to smile but fought to hide his amusement, aware that she wouldn't appreciate it. "I'm listening, Logan."

"Good. Because you have an agenda—that's clear enough—but it's not my agenda, and I'm not going to be bulldozed into going along with your plan."

He'd found her impossibly lovely three years ago, the night he'd spotted her at the auction. She had an intent gaze, focused and watchful, and in her delicate silver and periwinkle gown, she'd shimmered, her beauty mysterious…that of a remote, untouchable princess. The untouchable quality drew him in. He saw it as a challenge. He couldn't resist a challenge.

Now there was an entirely different challenge before him. A different woman. And he understood why she'd changed. She'd had to be everything for Jax—mother and father, protector and nurturer—and she'd done it truly alone, cut off from family, mocked by society, and the pressure and pain had stripped Logan down and reshaped her, giving her an edge, giving her strength. This woman standing before him was no doormat. This new woman exuded power and resolve. This new woman was sexual, too, dressed head to toe in black, the light of battle blazing in her eyes, illuminating her stunning features.

"I don't want to bulldoze you. That wouldn't be fair to you or our daughter."

He saw her tense when he said *our daughter*. "She is *our* daughter."

"She's not a bargaining chip."

"I would never make her one."

She rolled her eyes. "I don't believe that for a second

and neither should you. You are the most ruthless man I have ever met, Rowan, and that is saying a great deal considering my father is Daniel Copeland."

"I spent ten years in the military as an officer. I have nothing in common with your father."

"Don't kid yourself. Nothing stopped him from taking what he wanted. And nothing will stop you, either. You take what you want, when you want, and discard—"

"I didn't discard you."

Her eyes burned overbright. She swallowed once, and then again, struggling to hold back words.

He sighed inwardly. "I treated you badly, yes. But it won't be like that with Jax."

"You're right, it won't be, because she is not part of this…she is not part of us. She is herself, and lovely and everything that is best in the world, and I will protect her from those who'd hurt her, and that includes you, Rowan Argyros."

"You don't need to protect her from me."

"I wish I could believe that."

"I'm not a monster."

Logan looked away, lips compressing, a sheen of tears in her eyes.

His chest tightened and it felt as if somewhere along the way he'd swallowed rocks. They made his stomach hurt. He'd hurt her badly because he'd intended to hurt her, and the unfairness of it made him sick. But it wouldn't change the outcome of this conversation. He wasn't going to lose Jax.

And he wasn't going to lose Logan.

They'd be a family because it was the right thing. Because it was the best thing. Because it would keep both of them safe, and that was the world he knew best.

Safety. Security.

No one would get to them, no one could hurt them. He knew it, and in her heart, she had to know it, too.

Rowan rose and moved past her to drag the tapestry-covered armchair forward. "Sit, *mo chroí*. You'll be more comfortable, I promise you."

She shot him a derisive look. "You want me to sit because it will make me more passive. But I'm not interested in being passive or docile. I'm not interested in being managed or accommodating you in any way."

She wouldn't like it if she knew he found her so appealing right now.

She wouldn't like it if she knew how much he wanted to touch her. How much he wanted to cover her mouth and drink her in, tasting her, taking her, making her melt.

He could make her melt.

He could.

He could do it now, too. Even when she crackled and burned. It'd be easier now, when she was on fire, her temper stirred, because anger and passion were so very close, anger flamed passion, anger made passion explode...

Logan straightened and stepped away from the club chair, closing the gap between them. It only took that one step and he saw the flicker in her eyes and the bite of teeth into her soft lower lip.

She was not so indifferent, this fierce woman of his.

She was not unaware of the crackle and fire in the room and the tension pulsing between them.

He gazed down into her upturned face, her eyes wide and blue, her breathing ragged. He could even see the erratic pulse beating at the base of her throat. They were so very close. If he drew a deep enough breath his chest would touch hers.

If he shifted, his knee would find her thighs. He'd be

there between her thighs. He very much wanted to be between her thighs, too.

One touch and he'd have her.

One touch and she'd be his.

"I want you to sit," he said quietly, gently, his blood humming in his veins, his body taut, hard. "Because I'm very, very close to stretching you across my desk and having my way with you." He stared into her eyes, the faintest of smiles creasing the corners of his eyes, even as he let her see the challenge in his eyes, and allowed her to feel his leashed tension. She needed to know that things were getting serious. This wasn't a game. "But somehow I think you're not yet ready for us to pick up where we left off—"

"That's not even a possibility."

And then he did what he knew he shouldn't do, not because she'd resist him, but because it wouldn't help his position—that he was good for her and Jax, and that he was the right one to take care of them.

But there was something about Logan that made him throw caution to the wind and he was done with restraint. Clasping her face in his hands, he captured her mouth and kissed her deeply, kissing her with that heat and hunger he knew she responded to, and she did.

Her lips trembled beneath his and her mouth opened to him. His tongue stroked the inside of her lip and then in, finding her tongue and teasing her until he felt her hands on his arms, her grip tight. She leaned in, leaning against him, and she was so warm and soft and…his.

His, but not his. Because he still didn't understand why he felt so possessive about this woman. He didn't understand the attraction and wasn't even sure he wanted to be attracted. The fact that she could even test his control, provoked him.

"I could make you come right now," he murmured against her mouth, as aware of his erection straining against the fabric of his trousers as he was of the hot, honey taste of her on his tongue, "and you'd love it."

She stiffened but didn't pull away, her chest rising and falling against his own.

He'd offended her, and it'd been deliberate. Just like before, he lashed out at her when truthfully he was frustrated with himself.

So really, he was no different from three plus years ago.

God almighty.

Rowan let her go and stepped away. He hated himself just then.

What was he doing?

This wasn't like him. His career had been built on defending and rescuing others. He was a protector.

Except when it came to Logan.

Rowan went to his desk, rifling through papers, pushing aside a stack of folders, needing time to calm down and clear his head.

He needed to be able to think. He needed her to think. They both needed to make the right decisions. Decisions about marriage and the future. Decisions about where they'd raise Jax together, protecting Jax.

This wasn't about love, but responsibility.

And yet he'd fulfill his duty as a husband. He'd make sure Logan's needs were met. He'd be sure she was satisfied.

"You can't have me," she whispered, drawing a rough breath and taking an unsteady step back. "And you can't have Jax, either." She retreated another couple of steps, arms folded tightly over her chest. "Just because you swept us out of the country and deposited us here in your Irish estate, doesn't mean we're yours. We're not."

"*She* is."

"You didn't want her. You didn't want anything to do with us—"

"You never told me I was a father."

"I phoned. You mocked me. Scorned me."

"You keep talking about you. You never told me about her. What about *her*?"

A shadow crossed her face and Logan's expression shuttered. He'd scored a direct hit. She knew he was right.

He shrugged impatiently. "In your heart you know you gave up too easily. If you truly love her as much as you say you do, you should have fought for her rights. Fought to do what was best for her."

"You think you're best?" Her chin notched up and yet her full lips quivered, the soft full lower lip swollen from the hard, hot kiss. "You think you're father material?"

His jaw tightened. "It doesn't matter what you think. What matters is the law. As her biological father, I have rights, and I intend to exert those rights, and you can be part of our family, or—"

"There is no *or*, Rowan. I am her family."

"Just as I am her family, too."

"You said you wouldn't use her as a bargaining tool."

"Correct. I will not bargain for her. I will not bargain with her. I am claiming my rights, and my right to parent my daughter, and we can either do this together, making these decisions together, or we can take it to the courts and let them decide."

"You wouldn't win custody."

He gave her a long look. "Your late father is a crook... one of the greatest of this century. You've hidden my daughter from me—"

"You're twisting everything."

"But can't you see how this will play out in court? Can't

you see that you've been duplicitous? Every bit as deceit-ful as your father?"

"No."

"But yes, love, you have. Legally you have." He fell si-lent, and the silence stretched, heavy, weighted, pointed. She needed to face the truth, and in this case, she was wrong. The court would take issue with her choices. The court would penalize her for those choices.

Silence stretched and Logan's heart beat fast as she watched Rowan reach for another sheaf of papers, care-lessly flipping through them.

She continued to hold her breath as he leaned over and scrawled a few words—his signature maybe?—at the bot-tom of one page, and then flipped to another page and scrawled something again.

She hated this so much.

She hated bickering and fighting, especially when it was about a child. Her child.

And yes, Rowan was her biological father but it was im-possible to wrap her head around the fact that he wanted to be in Jax's life. That he wanted to be a true father.

Or maybe she was misunderstanding. Maybe he didn't want to be hands-on. Maybe this was about power…control.

"My father rarely spent time with his children," Logan said flatly, trying to hide the thudding of her heart and the anxiety rippling through her. "He spent his life at the of-fice. And then after the divorce, he saw Morgan, but not the rest of us. But that was because Morgan went to live with him, feeling sorry for him."

Rowan lifted his head, his gaze locking with hers. "But you didn't."

"It was his choice not to see us. Mother never kept us from him. He didn't care enough about us to maintain a relationship."

"But you view him as your father."

She struggled with the next words. "He paid our bills."

"So you really couldn't care less about him."

"I didn't say that."

"You want to attend his funeral."

"He was my father."

"Ah." Rowan dropped into his chair, and studied her from across the office. "And you don't think our daughter will care about her father? You assume she doesn't need one?"

"I never said that."

"But you've blocked me from her life. Kept her from knowing she has a father."

Logan closed her eyes and drew a slow breath. "There's a difference between paying for a child's expenses, and being engaged...and loving."

"And you assume I can only pay bills?"

Tension knotted her shoulders. Balls of ice filled her stomach. Logan flexed her fingers trying to ease the anxiety ricocheting inside her. After an endless moment she touched her tongue to her upper lip, dampening it. "You have assumed only the worst of me. You have judged me based on my name. You have treated me incredibly harshly, and it's difficult, if not impossible, to believe that you would want to be a father, much less a loving one."

"You were introduced to me as Logan Lane."

"Lane is my mother's name, and my preferred name. It is my name."

"Are you telling me you dropped the Copeland from your name?"

"I was in the process of legally changing my name. Yes. *Copeland* is a distraction."

He continued to study her, his expression impossible to read. He had such hard, chiseled features and his light eyes were shuttered. And then his mouth eased and his fierce expression softened. "No need to look so stricken. The good news is that we have the chance to fix things. You and I can sort this out without a judge…without the courts. It will be far less messy and painful if we manage our affairs privately. Surely you don't want your *distracting* name bandied about in the press? I would imagine that by now you've had enough media attention to last a lifetime."

Her stomach heaved. The very idea of being in the papers made her want to throw up. She couldn't bear to be chased again. It had been awful when the reporters and photographers shadowed her every move several years ago. She'd felt hunted. Haunted. And that was before Jax. No, Jax's picture could not be splashed about the tabloids. The reporters and photographers were merciless. They'd harass them, and terrify Jax by shouting at them, by pulling up in their cars, honking horns, creating chaos just to get a photo.

Logan exhaled slowly, clinging to her composure. "I have lived very quietly these past few years to stay out of the media."

"A custody battle will just put you right back in the headlines."

She stared at him, furious, frustrated, defiant.

His broad shoulders shifted. His gaze dropped to the papers in his hand. "The funeral has been set for a week from today. It will be held in Greenwich, Connecticut. Your sister Morgan is making the arrangements. Your mother and sisters will be there. It is hoped that you will be there, too." He looked at her once more. For a long moment he was silent before adding, "I hope we will be, but that is up to you."

"This is absurd."

"The grand service for your father...or that we'd attend together?"

"We're not a couple."

"Yet. But we will be."

"Many parents raise children in different homes—"

"Like mine," he interrupted. "And it was hell. I won't have my daughter—"

"Your daughter?" she interrupted bitterly.

"My daughter," he continued as if she hadn't spoken, "being dragged back and forth. It's unsettling for a young child. It's upsetting for an older child. We need to do better than that for her."

She hated that he was saying the very things that she believed to be true.

She hated that he was being the one who sounded responsible and mature.

Having grown up in a divorced family it wasn't what she wanted for Jax, but at the same time, she couldn't imagine a peaceful home, not if she and Rowan were living together in it. "It is better for a child to have two homes than one that is fraught with tension," she said tightly.

"That's why we need to put aside our differences and focus on Jax."

Logan looked away, a lump filling her throat. He made it sound so easy. He made it sound like a trip to an amusement park...but living with Rowan would be anything but fun. He'd hurt her so badly...he'd nearly broken her with his harsh rejection...

"I don't trust you," she whispered.

"Then I must win your trust back."

"That will take forever."

"We don't have that much time. The funeral is in a week."

She shot him a baffled glance. "I'm not sure I follow."

He dropped the papers and sat down in his chair. "We need to marry before the funeral because, if we're to go, we go united. You and me. A family."

*"What?"*

"We go united," he repeated firmly.

"There is no way…how could we possibly marry this week?"

"Not just this week, but tomorrow. That way we can slip away for a brief honeymoon before flying to Connecticut with Jax for the service."

"And if I refuse?"

"We stay here."

# CHAPTER SIX

*THEY'D STAY HERE?*

Logan's legs went weak. Boneless, she sank into the chair behind her. Her voice was nearly inaudible. "You'd keep me from his service?"

His gaze was cool, almost mocking. "I could say so many things right now...I could say you never told me you were pregnant. I could say you kept me from my daughter—"

"Yes. This is true. But two wrongs don't make a right."

"So, Logan *Lane*, make this right."

Her eyes stung. She blinked hard and bit hard into her lip to keep from saying something she'd regret.

The only thing that had kept her going these past three years when it had been so hard was the belief that one day her life would be different. That one day she and Jax would have everything they needed, that their future would be filled with hope and love and peace...

But there would be no peace with Rowan.

It wasn't the future she'd prayed for. It wasn't the future they wanted or needed.

It wasn't a future at all.

Rowan leaned forward, picked up a thick stack of glossy colored pages and held them out to her. "Pick one or two that appeal and they will be here later tonight."

She took the pages before she realized they were all

photographs of couture wedding gowns. Fitted white satin gowns that looked like mermaids and slinky white satin gowns with narrow spaghetti straps, and princess ballgowns with full skirts and gorgeous beading of pearls and precious stones…

The virginal wedding gowns were a punch in the gut and she nearly dropped the stack of designs before letting them tumble onto a nearby end table.

"We'll marry tomorrow night," he added, not sounding in the least bit perturbed by her reaction. "And steal away for a brief honeymoon, and then join your family in Greenwich."

"I'm not getting married like this. I'm not being forced into a marriage against my will."

"I don't want an unwilling wife, either. I want you to want this, too—"

"That's not going to happen."

"Not even for Jax?"

She took a step toward him and her gaze fell on the stack of bridal designs, the top one so outrageously fancy and fussy that it made her stomach cramp. "You don't know me. You know nothing about the real me. You and I would not be compatible. We weren't even compatible for one night—"

"That isn't true. We had an amazing night."

"It was sex."

"Yes, it was. Very, very good sex."

"But four hours or six hours of good sex isn't enough to justify a life together."

"Correct. But Jax is."

His reasonable tone coupled with his reasonable words put a lump in her throat. He was the bad guy. He was the one who'd broken her heart. How dare he act like the hero now?

She blinked away the tears and shook her head and headed for the door.

"We don't have a lot of time," he called after her. "If you won't pick a dress, then I'll have to select it for you."

She stood in the doorway, her back to him. "Your desire to protect Jax means crushing me," she said quietly. "And I know I don't matter to you, that I mean nothing to you, but you should be aware that I wanted more in life, and once I was a little girl, just like Jax, and on the inside, I am still that little girl, and that little girl within me deserves better."

Leaving his paneled study, she walked quickly down the long high-ceilinged hall and, spying an open door before her, went through that, stepping outside into the late afternoon light.

It was no longer raining but the sky was still gray, and the overcast sky turned the vast lawn and banked shrubbery into a landscape of shimmering emerald.

Logan descended the stone steps into the garden, feet crunching damp gravel. She began to walk faster down the path before her, and then she went faster, and then she broke into a run, not because she could escape, but because there was nothing else she could do with the terrible, frantic emotions clawing at her.

She dashed toward a stone fountain and then past that, focusing on the tall neatly pruned green hedges beyond. It wasn't until she was running through the hedges, making turn after turn, confusion mounting, that she realized it was a maze, and then abruptly her confusion gave way to relief.

It felt good to be lost.

There was freedom in being lost…hidden.

She slowed, but still moved, feet virtually soundless on the thick packed soil, so happy to be free of the dark castle with the thick walls and small windows…so happy to be far from Rowan's intense, penetrating gaze.

He didn't know her and yet he seemed to know too much about her, including the worst things about her… such as her weakness for him.

It was true that she couldn't seem to resist his touch, and it shamed her that she'd want someone who despised her. It shamed her that she despised him in return and yet she still somehow craved him.

This wasn't how it was supposed to be.

The physical attraction…the baffling chemistry…was wrong at so many levels.

She rounded a corner and nearly ran straight into Rowan. Logan scrambled backward. "How—" she started before breaking off, lips pinching closed because of course he knew his way about the maze. It was his maze.

His castle.

His world.

Her eyes burned. Her throat ached. She'd struggled for so many years, struggled to provide and be a strong mother, and now it was all being taken from her. Her independence. Her control. Her future.

She didn't want to share a future with him.

She didn't want to share Jax with him.

She didn't want anything to do with him and yet here he was, blocking her path, filling the space between the hedges, tall and broad, so very strong…

"What are you doing?" he asked, his brow furrowing, his expression bemused. "It's damp out. You don't have a coat."

"You've trapped me," she whispered, eyes bright with tears she wouldn't let spill because, God help her, she had to have an ounce of pride. "You've trapped me and you know it, so don't taunt me…don't. It's not fair."

And with a rough oath, he reached for her, pulling her against him, his body impossibly hard and impossibly warm as he shaped her to him. She shivered in protest. Or at least that's what she told herself when dizzying heat raced through her and the blood hummed in her veins, making her skin prickle and tingle and setting her nerves on fire, every one of them dancing in anticipation.

Her head tipped back and she stared up into his eyes, searching the green-gold for a hint of weakness, a hint of softness. There was none.

"I do not know what *fair* means," he said, his voice pitched low as his head dropped and his mouth brushed her temple and then the curve of her ear. "It's not a word that makes sense to me, but you, *mo gra*, you make sense to me when you shouldn't. You make me think that there is something bigger at work here."

"It's sex."

"Good. I like sex."

"It's lust."

"Even better." His lips brushed her cheek and then kissed the corner of her mouth. "I know what to do with that."

"But I want love, not lust." She put her hands on his chest, feeling the hard carved plane of the pectoral muscle and the lean muscular torso below. "I want selfless, not selfish. I want something other than what I've known."

"People are flawed. We are human and mortal and there is no perfection here. Just life." His mouth was on hers and he kissed her lightly and then again, this time the kiss lingered, growing deeper and fiercer, making her pulse jump and her body melt and her thighs press together because he was turning her on…again.

Again.

Just a touch and she ached. A kiss and she went hot and wet and everything in her shivered for him.

And when he bit at the softness of her lower lip, she knew that *he* knew. She knew that he understood her hunger and desire, and the worst part of all was that their history, that one torrid night, meant that she knew he could assuage it, too. But it burned within her, this physical weakness. It burned because she despised any weakness that would give Rowan the upper hand.

"I hate you," she whispered hoarsely.

"You don't." His hands twisted in her hair, tilting her head back, exposing her throat. His lips were on her neck and the frantic pulse beating beneath her ear. He kissed that pulse and then down, setting fire to her neck and the tender collarbone. "You don't hate me. You want me."

She gasped as his hand slid between them, fingers between her thighs, the heel of his palm against her mound.

And he was right. She did want him. But that only intensified her anger and shame.

She should be better than this. Stronger. Smarter.

Or at the very least, more disciplined.

Instead she let her eyes close and her body hum, blood dancing in her veins, making her skin warm and everything within her heat and soften.

She couldn't remember now why she'd found making love to him so incredible and so deeply satisfying, but her memory had clung to the pleasure, and his mouth on her skin was lighting fire after fire, making her legs tremble, dispatching what was left of her resistance.

"We can make this work without love," he said, his hand slowly sliding from her waist up her rib cage to just graze her breast.

She heard his words but they didn't compute, not when she was arching into his hand, longing to feel more, wanting the pressure of his fingers against her sensitive skin, wanting more friction everywhere to answer the wild heat inside of her.

"We don't have to be best friends to find pleasure with each other, either," he added. "We just have to agree that Jax comes first. And I think we can do that."

Then he kissed her so deeply that her brain shut up and her heart raced, silencing reason. She shouldn't want this, but she did. She shouldn't crave the intensity, and yet it ached and burned, demanding satisfaction. With their history, she should know that nothing good would come of this…sex would just be sex…and afterward she'd feel used and hollow, but that was the future and this was the present.

"So is that a yes?" he murmured against her mouth.

"No," she whispered, wanting the pleasure but not the pain.

"You want to be mine."

"No."

"You're mine already. You just need to admit it."

Her lips parted to protest but just then his hand brushed the swell of her breast and the words died unspoken. She shuddered, and the ripple of pleasure made her acutely aware of him. He was tall and muscular and hard. She could feel his erection straining against her. He wanted her. This…chemistry…wasn't one sided.

He brushed the underside of her breast again and she sighed, even as her nipple tightened, thrusting tautly against the delicate satin of her bra.

*"Rowan,"* she choked, trying to cling to whatever was left of her sanity, and yet the word came out husky and so filled with yearning that she cringed inwardly.

"Yes, *a ghra*?"

"This is madness. We can't do this—"

"But we already have. Now we just have to do right by our daughter." He released her, and drew back, his hard handsome features inexplicably grim. "So the only real question is, do you intend to select your bridal gown or am I to do it?"

With the distance came a breath of clarity. "I refuse to be rushed into marriage."

"We're short on time, Logan."

"We're not short on time. We have our entire lives ahead of us. Jax is so young she doesn't know the difference—"

"But *I* do. I want her to have what I didn't have, which is a family."

"No, you had a family. They were just dysfunctional... as most families are." Logan's voice sounded thin and faint to her own ears. She was struggling to stay calm, but deep down had begun to feel as if she was embroiled in a losing battle. Rowan was strong. He thrived on conflict. Just look at his career.

High risk, high stakes all the way.

"You are so focused on the end goal—getting Jax, being with Jax—that you don't realize you're crushing me!"

"I'm not crushing you. I'm doing my best to protect you. But you have to trust me—"

"I don't." Her voice sounded strangled. "At all."

"Then maybe that's what you need to work on."

*"Me?"*

He shrugged, as if compromising. "Okay, *we*. We need to work on it. Better?"

Back in her suite of rooms, Logan paced back and forth, unable to sit still. It was late, and Jax was asleep in the modified bed that had been assembled earlier against one wall of the huge walk-in closet, which had been turned into a bedroom for the toddler with the addition of a small painted chest, large enough to hold toddler-sized clothes, and provided a place for a lamp. It was a small, brass lamp topped with a dark pink shade that cast a rosy glow on the cream ceiling chasing away shadows and gloom. A framed picture of woodland fairies hung on the wall over the chest, giving Jax something to look at while in her snug bed. Rowan had even made sure Jax would be safe from falling out by adding a padded railing that ran the length of the bed.

But with Jax in bed for the night, Logan had far too much time to think and worry.

And she was worried.

She was also scared.

She was caught up in a sea of change and she couldn't get her bearings. She'd lost control and felt caught, trapped, pushed, dragged about as if she were nothing more than a rag doll.

But she wasn't a doll and she needed control. And if she had to share power, she'd share with someone she liked and admired and, yes, trusted.

Someone with values she respected.

Someone with integrity.

Rowan had no integrity. Rowan was little more than a soldier. A warrior. Great for battle but not at all her idea of a life partner…

Logan swallowed hard, trying to imagine herself wedded to Rowan. Trying to imagine dinners and breakfasts and holidays, never mind attending future school functions with him…

She couldn't see it.

Couldn't imagine him driving Jax to school or returning to pick her up or sitting in the little chairs for parent-teacher conferences. She couldn't see him being that father who was there. Present.

And then a lump filled her throat because maybe, just maybe, she didn't trust Rowan to love Jax because her father hadn't loved her. Maybe this wasn't about Jax at all—history was full of men who were good parents.

Logan had grown up surrounded by men who knew how to put their families first. Men who were committed and involved. She'd envied her classmates for having devoted fathers…fathers who routinely made it to their daughters' soccer games and dance recitals. Men who zipped up puffy jackets before they took their little girls outside into the cold. Men who'd put out an arm protectively when crossing a busy street. Men who didn't just show up in body but were there emotionally. Men who taught their daughters to ride bikes and drive cars and navigate life.

Logan's eyes stung. She held her breath, holding the pain in.

She'd wanted one of those fathers. She'd wanted someone to teach her about life and love and boys and men.

She'd wanted someone to tell her she was important and valuable. She'd wanted someone to say she deserved to be treated like a princess…like a queen…

Logan blinked, clearing her eyes.

But just because she didn't have a loving, attentive father, it didn't mean that Jax couldn't. Maybe Rowan could be a proper father. Maybe Rowan could teach Jax about life and love and boys…

And men.

Exhaling slowly, Logan glanced from the door of the closet—open several inches so she could keep an ear open in case Jax needed her—to the bedroom door that opened onto the castle hall.

She needed to speak to Rowan.

She didn't know what she'd say, only that she needed to speak to him about the whole marriage thing and family thing and understand what it meant to him. Was he going to be a father in name only or did he really intend to be part of Jax's life?

Because being a father had to be more than carrying on one's family name. Being a father meant *being* there. Being present. Being interested. Being patient. Being loving.

Logan peeked in on Jax and in the rosy pink glow she could see her daughter was fast asleep, her small plump hand relaxed, curving close to her cheek.

Jax's steady breathing reassured her. She was sleeping deeply. She shouldn't wake for hours—not that Logan would be gone hours. Logan planned to find Rowan and speak to him and then return.

She'd be gone fifteen minutes, if that. It'd be a short, calm conversation, and she'd try to see if they couldn't both discuss their vision for this proposed…marriage… and find some common ground, create some rules, so that when she returned to the bedroom she'd feel settled, and perhaps even optimistic, about the future.

At the foot of the staircase Logan encountered an unsmiling man in a dark suit, wearing a white shirt and dark tie.

"May I help you?" he asked crisply, revealing an accent she couldn't quite place.

"I was just going to see Rowan," she answered faintly, brow knitting, surprised to see someone so formally dressed at the foot of the stairs, and then understanding seconds later that he wasn't just anyone in a suit and tie, but a bodyguard…probably one of Rowan's own men. Which also meant he was probably armed and dangerous. Not that he'd pose a threat to her.

"Is he in his study?" she asked, nodding toward the corridor on the opposite side of the stairwell.

"He's retired for the night."

She didn't know how to respond to that, unable to imagine Rowan *retiring* from anything.

"His room is upstairs, just down from yours," the man added.

She knew where Rowan's room was. It was just on the other side of Jax's closet. The suite of rooms all had interior connecting doors, with the closet being shared by both bedrooms, but the door to Rowan's room had been locked and the chest of drawers had been placed in front of it, making the closet more secure.

It had been Rowan's suggestion.

He'd thought Logan would sleep better if she knew that no one could enter the room without her permission.

He was right. She did feel better knowing that the only way in and out of her suite was through the door to the hall, a door she could lock, a door she could control.

She'd been grateful for Rowan's understanding.

"Did he turn in a long time ago?" she asked.

"Quarter past the hour maybe. I can ring him for you, if you'd like."

"Not necessary," she answered lightly. "I can just stop in on my way back to my room."

She hesitated, glancing to the heavy front door across the entry hall.

She wondered just how far she'd get, if she ran for the door. Would she be allowed out? Somehow she suspected not. She sensed that this bodyguard wasn't just there to keep the bad guys out of Castle Ros, but to keep her and Jax *in*.

Rowan wasn't taking any chances.

And just like that she thought of Joe, and how Joe once upon a time must have been a bodyguard very much like this, a tall, silent man in a dark suit. That is, back before Rowan sent Joe to her, and Joe dropped the suit and intense demeanor to become her Joe, the recent college grad grateful to have a job…

Even though he was already employed, and apparently drawing two salaries. Her mouth quirked. She ought to speak to Joe about that.

"I'll head back upstairs," she said. "Good night."

His head inclined. "Good night."

And then she retraced her steps, footsteps muffled on the thick carpeting on the stone steps. The same carpet ran the length of the second-floor gallery with the corridor stretching east and west, marking the two wings of the castle.

Rowan opened his bedroom door just moments after she knocked, dressed in gray joggers and a white T-shirt that stretched tight across his chest and then hung loose over his flat, toned torso.

She couldn't help wondering if he'd been expecting her.

"Can we talk?" she asked.

He nodded and opened the door wider, inviting her in.

As she crossed the threshold, she flushed hot and then cold, her skin prickling with unease. She wasn't sure this was a good decision. She wasn't sure how she'd remain cool and calm if their conversation took place here.

As he closed the door, her eyes went to his oversize four-poster bed and then to the heavy velvet curtains drawn against the night. The room was close to the same size as hers and had the same high ceiling, but it felt far more intimate. Maybe it was the big antique bed. Or maybe it was the thick drapes blocking the moon. Or maybe it was the man standing just behind her, sucking all of the oxygen out of the room, making her head dizzy and her body too warm.

She drew an unsteady breath and turned to face him,

thinking she'd made a mistake. She shouldn't have ever come here, to him.

A tactical error, she thought. And worse, she'd voluntarily entered dangerous territory.

Swallowing her nervousness, she glanced to the chairs flanking the impressive stone hearth. "Can we sit?"

"Of course."

"It's not too late?"

"Not at all. I was just reading. I don't usually sleep for another hour or two."

Her gaze slid over the bed with its luxurious coverlet folded back, revealing white sheets.

She wanted to leave. She wanted to return to her room. It was all too quiet in here, too private. "Maybe it's better if we talk tomorrow. I'm sure you're as tired as I am—"

"Not tired yet. But I will be, later."

"I'm tired, though. Probably too tired to do this tonight. I just thought since Jax was asleep it might be convenient, but I'm worried now she'll wake and be scared..." Her voice drifted off and she swallowed, her mouth too dry.

He said nothing.

Her heart hammered harder. She felt increasingly anxious. He was so intense, so overwhelming. Everything about him made her nervous, but she couldn't tell him that. She couldn't let him know how powerless she felt when with him, and how that was bad, really bad, because she needed control. She needed to be able to protect herself. And Jax.

Logan grasped at Jax now, using her as an excuse to leave Rowan's room. "Let's schedule a chat for the morning. It would be best then. I wasn't thinking when I came here. I really don't want Jax to wake up and be frightened."

"I have security cameras. We'll know if she stirs. You'll be able to be at her side before she even wakes up."

Logan straightened, shocked. He had cameras? *Where?*
"You're watching our rooms?"

"I monitor the entire castle. There are cameras everywhere."

"You've been spying on us in our room?"

He sighed and crossed to a wall with dark wood paneling. Shifting a small oil landscape, he pushed a button, and
suddenly the wall split, opening, revealing a massive bank
of stacked TV screens. There had to be five screens across,
and five down, and some of the screens were blanks, while
others showed interior castle rooms and corridors, and others revealed exterior shots: entrances, garden paths and
distant iron gates.

She walked to the wall of monitors and searched for her
room with the pretty canopied bed, but the only thing she
could see was the closet door, slightly ajar, just as she'd
left it. And then she found another monitor showing the
hall outside her room.

No bed shots.

Nothing that indicated he was watching her. At least,
not until she'd exited her room and approached his.

So he could have known she was coming to see him.
He could have watched her leave her room and walk toward his.

She turned to face him. "You knew I was looking for
you. You saw me downstairs talking to the bodyguard."

"I knew you'd left your room. But I don't have the sound
on. I never do. It'd be too distracting."

"So you didn't know I was asking for you?"

"I thought maybe you wanted a snack."

She just stared at him, trying to decide if she believed
him or not. She wanted to believe him, but there was no
trust, and that was a huge problem. "So you closed the door
on the cameras when I knocked on your door?"

"Yes."

"You didn't want me to see them."

"I don't want anyone to see them. Security is my business."

"But you showed me."

"I thought you should know they are there. I thought you'd be reassured that Jax isn't alone or in danger."

"But if the door is closed on the screens, how do you monitor movement in the castle?"

"The cameras also alert me to movement, and I get those alerts on my computer, my phone and my watch."

"Can you turn those off?"

"I can disable them or mute them. Usually I just glance at the screen, note the alert and then ignore. I never disable them. It defeats the purpose of being secure."

She turned to pace before the fire.

Rowan said nothing for several minutes, content to just watch her. Finally he broke the silence. "What's on your mind, Logan?"

He didn't sound impatient. There was nothing hard in his tone and yet she felt as if she was going to jump out of her skin any moment now. "I thought maybe we could discuss your proposal," she said, unable to stop moving. Walking didn't just distract her, it helped her process, and it minimized her fear and tension. She didn't want to be afraid. She didn't want to make decisions because she was panicked. Those were never good decisions. "I thought we could see if we couldn't come to some agreement on the terms." She paused by the hearth, glanced at him. "Clarity would be helpful."

"The terms?" he repeated mildly. "It's not a business contract. It's a marriage."

She stiffened at the word *marriage*. She couldn't help it. It was one thing to imagine Rowan as a father to Jax, but another to consider him as her husband. "Relationships have rules," she said cautiously.

"Rules?"

She ignored his ironic tone and the lifting of his brow. The fact that he sounded so relaxed put her on edge. "Most relationships evolve over time, and those roles, and rules, develop naturally, gradually. But apparently we don't have time to do that, and so I think we should discuss expectations, so we can both be clear on how things would… work."

He just looked at her, green gaze glinting, apparently amused by every word that came from her mouth. His inability to take her seriously, or this conversation seriously, did not bode well for the future. "This isn't a game," she said irritably, "and I'm trying to have an adult conversation, but if you'd rather make a joke of this—"

"I'm not making a joke of anything. But at the same time, I don't think we have to be antagonistic the night before our wedding."

She shot him a fierce look. "We're not marrying tomorrow. There is absolutely no way that is going to happen tomorrow, and should we one day marry, we will not need a honeymoon. That is the most ludicrous suggestion I've heard yet."

"I thought all brides wanted honeymoons."

"If they're in love!" Her arms folded tightly across her chest. "But we're not in love, and we don't need alone time together. We need time with Jax. She ought to be our focus."

"An excellent point. Now please sit. All the marching back and forth reminds me of cadets on parade."

"I'll sit, but only if you do," she said, gaze locking with his. She wasn't about to let him score any points on her. She hadn't survived this long to be beaten by him now. Her father's betrayal and abandonment had been one thing, but to be betrayed and abandoned by her first lover? That had opened her eyes and toughened her up considerably.

"Happy to sit," he replied. "I imagine we will have many future evenings in here, in our respective chairs, you knitting, me smoking my pipe—"

"You don't smoke and I don't knit."

He shrugged. "Then we'll find another way to enjoy each other's company."

She was fairly certain she knew what he meant by *another way to enjoy each other's company*. He'd always been about the sex. Maybe that's because that was the only way he could relate to women. "You're being deliberately provocative."

"I'm trying to get you excited about the future."

"Mmm." She arched a brow. "Are you also going to sell me beachfront property in Oklahoma?"

"No. That's the kind of thing your father did. I'm honest."

Her jaw tightened, hands balling into fists. "You don't have to like him, but I ask you to refrain from speaking of him like that in front of Jax. She doesn't need to be shamed."

"I'm not shaming her. And I'm not shaming you, either—"

"Bullshit."

"I'm just not going to be fake. If I'm upset, I'll tell you. If I'm content, you'll know. And since we're going to raise Jax together, it's better if we're both forthright so there is no confusion about where things stand." He gave her a faint, ironic smile. "Or sit, since that was the whole point."

She shot him a look of loathing before crossing to the hearth and sitting down in one of the large leather chairs, watching as he followed and then took his time sitting down in the chair across from hers.

He smoothed his T-shirt over his lean, flat stomach before extending his legs and crossing them at the ankle, and then he looked up into her eyes and smiled.

"Better?" he asked.

She ground her teeth together. Rowan Argyros was enjoying himself immensely.

"My father was the breadwinner," she said flatly. "My mother was a homemaker. It meant that when they divorced, she still had to depend on him to provide. I will never do that. If we marry, I'm not giving up my career."

"When we marry, we won't end up divorced."

"I'm not giving up my career."

"You barely scrape by. I make millions every year—"

"It's your money. I want my own."

"I'll open a personal bank account for you, deposit whatever you want, up front, and it'll be yours. I won't be able to touch it."

"It will still be your money. I don't want your money. I'm determined to be self-sufficient."

"Why?"

She gave him a long look. "Surely you don't really have to ask that."

"You're the mother of my child. You've struggled these past few years to provide for her. Let me help."

"You can help with Jax's expenses. We will split them. Fifty-fifty."

"What if I provide for Jax and the family, and then you can use your own…money…for your personal expenses?"

She leaned forward. "Why do you say *money* like that?"

"Because you have virtually nothing in your bank account." He rolled his eyes, apparently as exasperated with her as she was with him. "I'm not hurting financially. According to the *Times*, I'm one of the wealthiest men in the UK. I can afford to make sure you're comfortable."

"My work gives me an identity. It gives me purpose."

"Being a mother doesn't do that?"

"This isn't about being a mother. It's about being a woman, and I don't want to be a woman who depends on a man. My mother spent her life living in my father's shadow, and as we both know, he cast a pretty big shadow. I don't want to be defined by a man, and I like being able to contribute to the world."

He said nothing and she added more quietly, a hint of desperation in her voice. "Work makes me feel valuable. It tells me I matter." She looked away, throat working, emotion threatening to swamp her. "I need to matter. I must matter." Her eyes found his again. "Otherwise, what's the point?"

"But you do matter. You're the sun and moon for Jax. You're her everything."

"And what if something happens to Jax? What if—God forbid—there was a tragedy, and I lost her? I'd be lost, too. I'd be finished. There would be nothing left of me." Her voice cracked but she struggled to smile. She failed. "She's everything."

"Nothing is going to happen to her," he said gruffly. "Why would you think that?"

She couldn't answer. She bit down into her lip, her heart on fire, because bad things did happen. Her parents had divorced when she was young and her father had virtually forgotten her and then later it turned out that he was a criminal...he'd stolen hundreds of millions of dollars from his clients...

"Nothing is going to happen," Rowan repeated more forcefully.

She nodded, but tears were filling her eyes and she was pretty sure that she hadn't convinced either of them of anything.

For a long minute it was quiet. Logan knit her fingers together in her lap, knuckles white. Rowan didn't say anything, deep in thought. She glanced at him several times, thinking he'd lost the glint in his eyes, aware that his hard features had tightened, his mouth now flattened into a grim line.

She couldn't handle the silence any longer. "Maybe I shouldn't feel that way. Maybe it seems irrational—"

"It doesn't." His voice, pitched deep, cut her short.

She looked at him, surprised.

His broad shoulders shifted. "My little brother's death destroyed my mother, and it ended my parents marriage."

"You lost a brother?"

He nodded. "I was seven. Devlin was two, nearly three."

*Jax's age.*

He knew what she was thinking. She could see it in his eyes.

"But that won't happen to Jax," he added roughly, his voice as sharp as ground glass. "I will make sure nothing happens to her. And that's a promise."

She couldn't look at him anymore, couldn't stomach more of the same conversation. Jax was so valuable. Jax was perfect and innocent, not yet hurt by life or other people. She didn't yet know that people—even those who claimed to care about you—would fail you. Hurt you. Maybe even deliberately hurt you.

Logan hadn't remained a virgin so long because she didn't have options. Her virginity wasn't kept because there weren't men available but because she wanted to hold part of herself back. She wanted to save herself for the right person. She'd wanted to give that one thing—that bit of innocence—to a man who'd value her.

How she'd gotten that wrong!

Being disappointed was a fact of life. Learning to deal

with that disappointment, another critical life lesson. And it was fine to learn about life, and have to accept loss and change, but far better if those lessons came later. If the individual self was shaped and formed. Strong.

"You and I can make sure Jax is safe," Rowan said quietly, drawing her attention to him. "With vigilance we can give her the life I know you want for her."

Logan blinked tears away. "What life do I want for her?"

His gaze held hers for an extra long moment. "You don't want her crushed. You don't want her broken. You want her to remain a child as long as possible—safe, loved, cherished." He hesitated, and the silence hung there between them, weighted. "You want to give her the childhood you never had."

His words cut, pricking her when she didn't have the proper defenses. Startled, uncomfortable, she left her chair, crossing the floor a ways to stand before the bank of monitors. Jax's door remained ajar, just as she'd left it. She suddenly wished she could see Jax, though. She wanted to be sure the little girl was still soundly sleeping.

"Do you have sound, if you wanted it?" she asked thickly, keeping her back to him even as the threat of tears deepened her voice.

"Yes."

"Can you turn it on in her room? Or in my room? So we can check to see if it's quiet or if she's crying?"

"I could turn the camera in her room on. If you'd like?"

She glanced at him now. "So there is a camera in the closet?"

"I disabled it earlier, but I can turn it on."

"I didn't see one in the closet. Where is it?"

"It's positioned in the crown molding, hidden in the shadows of the woodwork."

"It's very small then?"

"No bigger than the head of a writing pen."

"Are cameras truly manufactured that small?"

"Mine are."

"You make cameras?"

He shrugged. "One of my companies manufactures cameras and security equipment. These small cameras are now used all over the world, in every big hotel, casino, government building." He crossed to her side, tapped several buttons on a panel and suddenly one of the dark screens came to life, and then he tapped another key on the panel and she could see Jax in her little bed, still sound asleep, although she now lay on her back, arms up by her head.

Logan shot him a troubled look. "I hate that you can spy on us."

"I don't spy on you. I haven't spied on you ever."

"Joe…?"

"Protection. And the cameras that remain are for protection.

"I deactivated all of the cameras in the closet, the bathroom, the bedroom, but the one positioned on the closet door. I thought it was important to know if Jax wandered out."

Logan shot him another assessing look. "Or if someone wandered in."

"Yes."

"Does that include me?"

"You're her mother."

"Which is why you're afraid I might try to run away with her."

He made a soft, tough mocking sound. "It's crossed my mind," he agreed. "More than once."

The smiling curve of his firm mouth just barely reached his eyes. His green gaze wasn't as warm as it was challenging. She didn't understand what she saw, didn't understand the tension or emotion...if it was emotion. But then he was an enigma, and he had been from the start.

That night at the auction he'd given her the same look—long, searching, challenging.

He'd looked at her with such focus that he didn't seem to be standing across the room, not part of the auction, but all by himself, and it was just the two of them in the room.

Everyone fell away that night in March.

The music, the sound, the master of ceremonies at the microphone.

There was just Rowan standing on the side of the stage looking at her, making her go hot and cold and feel things she didn't know a stranger could make her feel.

"And why would I run from you?" she asked, her chin lifting, her voice husky. She wasn't going to be the one to break eye contact. She wasn't going to back down. Not from him, not from anyone.

"Because you know when I take you to bed, it'll change everything. Again."

Her stomach flipped and her head suddenly seemed unbearably light, as if all the blood had drained away. "That's not happening." Thank God her voice was relatively firm because her legs were definitely unsteady.

"You sound so sure of yourself."

"Because I know myself. And I know you now, and I know how devastating it would be to go to bed with you—and not because you're good in bed, but because you're cruel out of bed, and I don't need more cruelty in my life."

"That was three years ago."

"Perhaps, but standing here with you, it seems like yesterday."

He shrugged. "I can't change the past."

"No, you certainly cannot."

And then he was reaching out to lift a heavy wave of hair off her face, his palm brushing her cheek as he pushed the hair back, slipping it behind her ear. "But I can assure you the future will be different."

His touch sent a shiver coursing through her. "I don't want—" she started to say before breaking off, because he was still touching her, his fingers sweeping her cheekbones, his fingertip skimming her mouth, making it tingle.

"Mmm?" he murmured, eyebrow lifting. "I'm listening, love."

She stared up into his eyes, her heart racing even faster, beating in a hard, jagged rhythm that made it difficult to catch her breath, much less speak. But how could she speak when her thoughts were scattered, coherent thought deserting her at the slightest touch?

"You know," he said thoughtfully, combing her hair back from her face to create a loose ponytail in one hand, "I never asked you about relationships you might have left behind…is there someone significant…?"

He was seducing her with his touch. She couldn't resist the warmth, couldn't resist the tenderness in his touch. She hated that she responded to his caress this way, hated that she felt starved for affection. He wasn't the right man for her. He'd never be the right man. "No."

"Why not? You're young and stunning—"

"And a mother with a young child dependent on me."

"You didn't want to meet someone…someone who could help you, make things easier for you?"

*"No."*

"Why not?"

"Surely it doesn't surprise you that I don't have a lot of confidence in men? That the men I've known—" she gave him a significant look "—cared only for themselves, too preoccupied by their own needs and their own agendas to take care of anyone else."

"You're not describing me."

"Oh, I most certainly am."

"Then you don't know me, and it's time to change that. Starting now. Tonight."

# CHAPTER SEVEN

HE CAPTURED HER MOUTH with his, shaping her to him. The kiss had fire and an edge that revealed far more of his emotional state than he preferred her to know, but right now he was damned if he cared about anything but taking what he wanted. And he wanted her.

He would bed her tonight.

He would claim her as his.

He wondered if she even realized that she didn't stand a chance because, now that she was here at Castle Ros, he wasn't about to lose her.

He'd made the mistake once. He wouldn't make the same once twice. And, no, his feelings weren't tender or loving, but passion and possession didn't require love. Passion and possession needed heat, and there was plenty of that.

"Mine," he murmured against her mouth, making her heart race.

She heard him but couldn't decipher it, not when heat flooded her, making her weak.

His kiss did this to her. His kiss turned her inside out, confusing her, making her forget who she was and why they didn't work…

Because right now they did work. Right now he tasted like life and hunger and passion, and she wanted more, not less. And no, it wasn't safe, but she hadn't lost control in years…not since she was last with him…and suddenly she was desperate to be his…desperate to feel him and know him and remember why she'd given herself to him.

What had made him the one?

He shaped her to him, his powerful body hard against her and his mouth firm, nipping at her lip, parting her lips, tasting her. He wanted more from her, too. More response. More heat. The insistent hunger of his kiss made her head dizzy and legs tremble.

She clung to him, feeling one of his hands at the swell of her breasts. She shuddered and then shuddered again as he cupped her breast, sending sensation rushing through her. She made a hoarse sound of pleasure and he practically growled with satisfaction.

She felt his hands on the hem of her sweater, lifting the hem and tugging it up over her head, and then he was at the waistband of her trousers, tugging the zipper down before glancing at her feet and noticing the boots. He pushed her back onto the bed so that he could remove one boot and then the other, and then the trousers were gone, leaving her in just her bra and matching pantie.

She reached for his coverlet, wanting to hide, but he leaned over her, pinning her hands to the mattress.

"I want to look," he growled, his voice deepening, his Irish accent becoming pronounced.

She felt shy and she closed her eyes, but even with her eyes closed she could feel his burning gaze, which drank her in the way a parched man drinks a tall, cool glass of water.

His head dipped, and his lips brushed her jaw and then the column of her throat.

Air bottled in her lungs and her toes curled as he kissed down her throat to the hollow between her collarbones.

She shouldn't like this so much. She shouldn't want his mouth and his tongue and his skin...but she did.

She loved his firm grip on her wrists and the way he pinned her to the bed, his body angled over hers, his knees on the outside of her thighs.

His mouth trailed lower, his lips between her breasts and then light on the silky fabric of her bra, his breath warm through the delicate fabric, teasing the pebbled nipple with the lightest scraping of teeth, making her arch up, and her hips shift restlessly.

He worked his way to the other breast, teeth catching at the edge of the bra, and then sliding his tongue along the now-damp fabric, his tongue tracing the line of her bra against her skin.

She could feel the rasp of his beard and the heat of his mouth and as erotic as it was, it wasn't enough.

Her hips rocked up. She felt hot and wet and empty.

He could fill her. He should fill her. Hard. Fast. Slow and fast.

Anything, everything.

"You know what I want," she whispered, licking her upper lip because her mouth had gone so dry.

His head lifted, and he gazed down at her. "And you know what I want," he answered.

"I want sex and you want a wife." She'd meant it bitterly but her voice was so husky the words came out breathless. "Something seems wrong here."

"It's easy to have sex. It's harder to find the right wife."

"I'm not the right wife."

"You are now."

"Because of Jax."

"Because of Jax," he agreed, head lowering, his mouth capturing one taut nipple and sucking hard on the sensitive tip.

He worked the nipple until she was writhing and panting beneath him.

"Rowan, Rowan—"

"Yes, *mo chroi*?"

"You're torturing me."

"Just as I will torture you every night in my bed." He blew on the damp silk of the bra, warm air across the pebbled nipple. "I'm going to do this to your pussy, until you come."

"Rowan. I want you in me."

"I know you do, but I'm not ready to give you what you want. I think you need to be punished—"

"For what?"

"Where do I start?" He bit down on the nipple making her cry out. "You should have told me who you were… you should have told me you were a virgin…you should have told me you were pregnant…" He looked down at her, green-gold eyes blazing. "Should I go on?"

"But that's it. That's all. There's nothing else I've done wrong."

"So you admit you were wrong."

Her eyes closed as she felt his hand on her hip, caressing the hipbone. "I could have been better at communicating," she whispered, pulse racing, thinking she should tell him to stop even though she didn't want him to stop.

And then his hand was between her thighs, cupping her mound, the heel of his palm pressing against her, filling her with hot sharp darts of sensation, and his mouth was taking hers again, all heat and honey and mind-drugging pleasure.

She'd wanted him that first night they'd met, and oh, she wanted him again now. Maybe even more because she knew how good he felt, his body buried deep in hers, making her body come to life with each maddening thrust, the slow deep strokes making her hope and want and feel, and she'd cling to him just as she had then, and for those moments they were joined, there was nothing else she needed...

And then his head lifted and his heavy-lidded green-gold gaze searched hers. "You want me."

It was impossible to deny when her arms were now wrapped tightly around his neck. "Yes."

"You need me."

Her body was on fire. "Yes."

"But you don't like me, you don't trust me and you won't marry me."

"We don't know each other. We're just...good in bed."

The corner of his mouth lifted. "But it's a start."

"We can't base a marriage on sex!"

His broad shoulders shifted and yet his eyes bored into hers. "There are plenty of couples who don't even have that."

A lump filled her throat. She loved the feel of him against her, the weight of his muscular body and the heat of his chest where it rested on hers and she dug her fingers into the short, crisp strands of hair at his nape and tugged. "I'm tired of being grateful for small mercies."

"Sometimes all we get are small blessings."

Her heart did a painful thump. "I want more." It hurt to speak but she forced herself to add, "I refuse to settle for less."

And then after a long moment where she felt as if he was staring deep into her soul, his head dropped and he was kissing her again, his hand sliding around to unfasten the hook on her bra and peeling it away. His lips captured an exposed nipple, and her breath caught in her throat as he licked the tip, making it wet and then moving to the other nipple. The combination of warm wet mouth and then cool air made her belly clench and her thighs press tight. She tugged on his hair, holding him to her breast, as he began to suckle harder.

It was impossible to silence her husky groan of pleasure, impossible to not lift her hips to find his. She needed more from him. She needed all of him.

She'd gone years—three years—without his touch... without any touch from any man...and yet now, together like this, she felt as if she'd shatter if she didn't have him tonight.

He was peeling off her panties, dragging the scrap of satin down her bare legs and then tugging off his own T-shirt and joggers.

His erection sprang free and her gaze went to his torso with the sculpted muscle, the hard taut abdomen, the corded thighs and of course, the thick, long shaft at full attention.

The air caught in her throat as she took him in.

He was beautiful.

Her first. Maybe her last.

It didn't make sense and yet in some ways, it was exactly as it should be. She'd lost her head over him, giving him not just her virginity but her heart.

And she had given him her heart.

She'd fallen for him hard, so hard, and she'd imagined that he'd cared for her, thinking it was impossible to make love the way they had without feelings being involved...

She'd been sure there were feelings, the lovemaking so intense it'd felt somehow as if they were soul mates. Perfect and perfectly made for each other.

And now, here they were, three years older and wiser and yet she still craved the feel of his mouth and the taste of him and the feel of him...

"Look at you, such a bold thing," he drawled, shifting over her, his knees pushing between hers, making room for him between her thighs. "Getting an eyeful, are you?"

Her lips curved faintly. "There's a lot to look at."

"Disappointed?"

"You know you've got the…goods."

"Small blessings, *mo chroi*."

"I wouldn't say small in this case." She reached out and touched his rigid length. He was warm and silken and hard all at the same time. She heard his sharp inhale as she stroked the length of him so she did it again. He pulsed in her palm, straining against her. Just the feel of him made her ache on the inside. "Definitely not small."

His eyes gleamed as he lowered himself to kiss the valley between her breasts and then down her rib cage to her belly. He'd slipped a hand between her thighs, parting them wider and giving him access to her delicate skin and tender pink folds.

Logan sucked in a breath as he found her, gently exploring her sex, and she was ready for him, already so wet. Her eyes closed as she felt his hands moving, touching, stirring her up, making her shiver.

She was ready for him, so wet, and she could feel him slipping a teasing finger over her dampness and then tracing the softness, lightly dragging the moisture up over silken skin to her sensitive nub. He knew just how to touch her and the pressure of his finger against her clit made her heart pound. Sparks of light filled her head while honey poured through her veins…

He kissed her taut, tense belly as he stroked her, and then he kissed down her abdomen, until he was parting her inner lips to lick the tender clit. She gasped as his tongue flicked across her, making her go hot and cold. The pleasure of his mouth on her was so intense it was almost painful. Her toes curled and she buried her hand in his hair, her breath coming faster, shorter as he pressed fingers into her core, finding that invisible spot that heightened sensation. He thrust deeper into her, stroking that spot as he sucked on her nub and did it again and again so that she couldn't hang on to a single rational thought, her body no longer her body but his to play with and control.

Logan dragged in great gulps of air as he brought her closer and closer to orgasm. She dug one heel into the bed, trying to resist, doing her best to hold off from climaxing, in part because she wasn't ready for something so intense, but also because it felt so amazing she wasn't ready for it to end. But Rowan wasn't about to let her escape. He was far too clever with his fingers, and he knew how to control her with his mouth and teeth and tongue, and then the tip of his tongue flicked over her so slowly that she broke, the orgasm so intense that she almost screamed, but caught herself in time. Tears filled her eyes instead.

Hell.

He took her to heaven and then dropped her into hell.

It wasn't supposed to be this way. It wasn't supposed to feel this way. She shouldn't want him when he'd wounded her so deeply.

And then he was stretching next to her, his large powerful body pulling her close, and he kissed her, deeply, and even though he'd yet to bury his body inside her, she knew he was staking claim. His hands cupped her face, his mouth drank her in.

*Mine*, his fierce carnal kiss seemed to say. *You belong to me.*

But then he was drawing back, and he studied the tears slipping from her eyes. "What hurts?" he asked.

She looked up into his eyes. It was hard to breathe when

it felt as if a concrete block rested on her chest. It took her forever to answer. "My heart."

He held her gaze for another long moment and then his head dropped and his lips brushed hers. "Hearts heal." And then, kissing her, he shifted his weight, his hips wedged between her thighs.

She felt the thick smooth head of his shaft against her, pressing at her entrance and it felt good. He felt good.

She hated that.

She wished she could tell him to get lost, to go screw himself, to leave her alone but she didn't want that. She didn't want him anywhere but here, against her, with her.

"You make me want to hate you," she choked even as his thick rounded tip just pressed inside her body. She was wet and he was so warm and smooth and even though the tip was just barely inside her, intense pleasure rippled through her. It was the most exquisite sensation, him with her.

"You hate me because you like it so much," he answered, nipping at her neck, finding more nerves, creating more pleasure.

He was right. She shouldn't welcome his touch when she didn't like him, but separating sensation and reason was impossible when he was close to her. Something happened when he was near…something so intense it was like a chemical reaction.

He was a drug.

Potent. Dangerous.

Like now.

He was there at her entrance, the tip just barely inside her. He didn't thrust deeper. He didn't even move his body. And yet her body was going wild, squeezing him, holding him, desperate to keep him with her, in her.

"So hate me," he murmured, slipping in just another inch, if that. "I don't mind."

Her body pulsed. She struggled to get air into her lungs. Her skin felt so hot that she wanted to rip it off.

"You love this," she gritted, her nails raking his shoulders.

"I love that I can make you feel so good."

"If you really wanted me to feel good, you'd do something."

"I think you're feeling really good right now."

She didn't know about that. Her body felt wild. Her inner muscles were convulsing, squeezing the thick rounded tip of his shaft, again and again. She'd never felt anything like this and she couldn't figure out if she loved it or hated it, so hard to know what she wanted when everything within her was so turned on.

"It's not enough," she said breathlessly.

"What would you like then?"

"You know."

And he did know, because he did it just then, thrusting hard into her body, seating himself deeply.

She nearly groaned out loud. *This*…this was what she wanted. Her arms wrapped around his shoulders and she held him tightly to her, her eyes burning and her throat aching because she felt overwhelming emotion…

She'd missed him somehow.

She had.

Even though he'd broken her heart, she'd missed him and this…

And the tears seeped from beneath her lashes, as she struggled to contain the emotion and the pain.

"Don't cry, *mo chroi*," he said, shifting his weight to his forearms to pull out and then thrust in again, slowly, deeply. "It's not bad to feel good. Let me make you feel good."

Her head knew everything about this was dangerous.

Everything would just fall apart later but right now she couldn't think clearly. She had no defenses against this… against him. He made her come alive. He made her feel. Her spine tingled. Her skin prickled.

"Make me feel good then," she whispered, giving in.

He began to move, burying himself deeply just to draw back out, his length so warm inside of her. Each thrust brushed against that sensitive spot within her, and each thrust put pressure on her clit, so that he stroked nerve endings inside and outside and there was no way to resist the tension coiling within her. It was just a matter of time before she'd come again.

It was just a matter of time before he'd make her shatter again.

His tempo increased, and his body thrust harder, faster, and she clung tighter, answering each thrust with a lift of her hips, pressing up against him to create the most tension and friction.

He growled his pleasure, and from his quickening tempo, she knew he was close to coming but he held back for her, determined to give to her, and she wanted to hold back just to defy him…it seemed so important to defy him…but his hand moved between them and he was stroking her clit and there was no resisting him. She climaxed just seconds before he did and he bore down on her, driving into her, filling her with his seed.

It was only then that her little voice whispered, *This is how one gets pregnant*…

Of course.

A great way to trap her was to put another baby into her womb. Give them another life to protect.

She didn't want to cry now. She wanted to hit him. Fight him.

"You may have made me pregnant," she said hoarsely

as he shifted his weight, settling onto his side on the mattress next to her.

"Yes," he answered, pulled her onto her side so that he could hold her close to his chest, his long legs tangling with hers.

She stiffened. "That's not a good thing."

"Jax would like a brother or a sister."

"How can you say that?" She struggled to sit up but he didn't let her escape. "You don't even know her!"

He shrugged, his arms like iron bands. "All kids benefit from a sibling."

And then when he said no more, she glanced back at him and his eyes were closed, his long lashes resting on his high cheekbones. His even breathing told her he was already asleep.

She told herself she'd never be able to sleep like this. She told herself it would be impossible to relax. How could she doze off when her mind was racing? And yet somehow, minutes later, she was asleep, still captive in Rowan's muscular arms.

# CHAPTER EIGHT

ROWAN LAY AWAKE, Logan sleeping at his side. He'd been awake for the past hour, listening to her breathe and thinking about the night.

It'd been years since he'd felt so much hunger and need, years since he'd wanted a woman the way he wanted Logan tonight.

Just remembering the lovemaking made him hard all over again. He'd found such erotic satisfaction in the shape of her, the softness of her skin, the scent of her body, the intensity of her orgasms.

He loved the taste of her and the urgency of her cries as she climaxed.

He hadn't felt this way about a woman since…

The March 31 when he'd first bedded Logan Lane.

The corner of his mouth pulled and he lightly stroked her hair where it spilled across his chest.

She wanted things he couldn't give her—romance, love—but he could give her other things, important things…stability, security, permanence.

He wasn't going anywhere. He wouldn't abandon her. He'd never betray their daughter, either.

And just because he couldn't give love, that didn't mean their relationship had to be empty or cold. This physical connection was hot. There was no reason they couldn't enjoy the heat and pleasure. They should take pleasure in each other. There would be no other.

Marriage was a commitment. He would be committed. Love wasn't necessary. In fact, love was a negative. It added pain and unnecessary complications. They didn't need the emotion. He didn't need it, and she'd be fine without it, too.


Logan woke and for a moment she didn't know where she was.

The bed was strange. Huge and imposing with its monster antique four-poster frame—and yet the white sheets were so soft and smooth they felt delicious against her skin.

Stretching, her body felt tender. Between her thighs it felt very tender.

And then she remembered it all. Rowan's mouth on her. His cock filling her. His expertise that made her come once, and then again.

And in the next moment she remembered Jax and she glanced at the wall of monitors to check the camera in Jax's room, but the screens were dark. The monitors were turned off.

Logan flung herself from bed, panicked. She grabbed the nearest piece of clothing—Rowan's T-shirt—pulled it over her head and raced back to her room. The curtains were open, sunlight poured through the tall, narrow windows, the sky beyond a hopeful blue.

Jax's bed in her closet bedroom was empty.

Logan tried to calm herself, knowing that in this place nothing bad would happen to Jax. The Irish nanny, Orla, probably had her. They were undoubtedly playing fairy-something somewhere, but until Logan saw Jax, and knew without a doubt that Jax was safe, Logan couldn't relax.

She stepped into shorts and dashed from her room, running down the stairs by two.

There were no bodyguards at the foot of the stairs today. The huge stone entry was empty. She went to Rowan's study. That was empty, too.

Where was he? Where was everyone? Had Rowan taken Jax and gone? Leaving her here?

She retraced her steps, returning to the impressive staircase but turning left instead of right and kept going until she reached the castle's kitchen. It was a cavernous vaulted space made of stone and dramatic arches. The huge commercial oven was tucked into what once must have been a medieval hearth, and a bank of tall, sleek stainless-steel refrigerators took up another wall. The kitchen was warm and smelled of yeast and warm bread. A woman had been bent over in front of the wood-topped island and now straightened. Startled by the appearance of Logan, she plunked her mixing bowl of rising dough on the island and wiped her hands clean on a nearby dish towel. "Hello. Can I help you with something?"

"My daughter," Logan said urgently. "I can't find her."

"Your little one is with Mr. Argyros." She turned to the stove, and pulled out a tray of golden scones and then another and placed them on top of the stove. "You'll find them outside in the garden." The cook nodded toward the garden beyond the kitchen door. "You can go that way. It's quickest."

"Thank you."

The air was cool and the gravel path hurt her feet. She should have worn shoes but Logan wasn't going back until she found Jax. She hurried down the path, trying not to shiver, telling herself there was no need to be afraid, but what if Jax was scared and Rowan wasn't patient? What if Jax was in one of her toddler moods—

She stopped short as she rounded the corner.

There between the hedges and the castle's kitchen herb garden was a little round table with matching painted chairs. A delicate lace cloth covered the pale blue wooden table and in one chair sat Jax, a tiny crown on top of her head, and in the other sat Rowan, looking beastly big in his pixie-sized chair. He was holding a miniature china cup and Jax was reaching for her cup and beaming up at him as if she was a real princess and Rowan her prince.

Logan couldn't breathe. She'd never seen Jax look at anyone like that. Not even Joe, whom she adored.

Logan's pulse still raced but her heart felt unhinged, flip-flopping around inside of her, hot emotions washing through her, one after another.

They were having a tea party in the garden. A father-daughter tea party.

And not just a casual affair, but this one had an arrangement of purple pansies in a little milk pitcher, and a silver tiered tray of sweets filled with little iced cakes and fragrant golden scones.

Someone had gone to a great deal of effort. Had Orla planned this? It seemed to be the sort of thing a professional nanny would think of, and yet there was something about the way the pansies spilled out of the pitcher that made Logan think this wasn't Orla, but someone else…

Her gaze settled on Rowan. He was smiling at Jax, his expression infinitely warm and protective. Doting, even.

Logan's eyes burned and she struggled to get air into her lungs but she couldn't see and she couldn't think, not when she was feeling so much.

Rowan looked like a giant in the small blue chair, his shoulders immense, drawing his shirt tight across his broad back, while the fine wool of his black trousers outlined his muscular thighs.

But Jax wasn't the least bit intimidated by the size of Rowan. If anything, she was delighted with her company, beaming up at Rowan as she sipped her tea, her chubby fingers clutching the little cup before she set it back down to ask if he needed more tea.

He nodded and Jax reached for the pot to top off his cup. As she started to pour the tea, she noticed her mother, set the pot down with a bang, and waved to Logan. "Mommy!"

"Hello, sweet girl," Logan said, blinking away tears before Jax could see them.

"We're having a party!" Jax cried, reaching up to adjust her tiara. "I'm a princess."

"Yes, you are." Logan walked toward their little table, but avoided Rowan's gaze. He was too much of everything.

Jax frowned at her mother's bare legs. "Where are your clothes, Mommy?"

"I need some, don't I?"

"Yes. You look naked." Jax sounded scandalized.

"I know, and it's a princess party. I'm terribly underdressed. I'm sorry."

Logan leaned over and dropped a kiss on her daughter's forehead. "Is that real tea you're drinking?"

Jax nodded vigorously. "Yes."

"If apple cider is tea," Rowan replied, his voice pitched low, but even pitched low she heard the amusement in it.

She darted a glance in his direction, not sure what to expect, but thinking he'd be smug this morning, after last night.

Instead his expression was guarded. He seemed to be gauging her mood.

Logan wished she knew how she felt. Everything was changing and she felt off balance and unable to find her center. "Is this her breakfast?" she asked, noting the little cakes and miniature scones on the tiered plate taking center stage on the table.

"It's *tea*, Mommy," Jax said sounding a bit exasperated. "Breakfast was at breakfast." She then looked at Rowan, and her expression softened, her tone almost tender as she asked him, "More tea?"

"I haven't drunk my last cup," he answered Jax regretfully.

"Then drink it." Jax turned back to her mother, earnestly adding, "We only have two cups. Sorry, Mommy."

Logan couldn't help thinking that Jax didn't seem the least bit sorry that her mother couldn't join them. The little girl was soaking up the attention. "That's okay. I should probably go dress." But Logan found it hard to walk away. The party was so charming and Jax had never not wanted her company before. It was new, and rather painful, being excluded.

Rowan glanced at her, looking almost sympathetic. "You don't have to leave. We can find you a chair, if you'd like."

The fact that he seemed to understand her feelings made it even worse. He wasn't supposed to be the good guy. He was the bad guy. And yet here he was, dressed up in black trousers and a white dress shirt, balancing himself in a pint-size chair, and drinking apple cider in a cup about the size of a shot glass.

"How nice of Orla to arrange this," she said, injecting a brisk cheerful note into her voice. "I'll have to thank her when I see her."

"Orla won't be here for another half hour," Rowan answered.

Logan frowned, confused. "But she made arrangements for the tea, yes?"

"No," he said.

"My daddy did," Jax said, casting another loving look on Rowan.

*Her daddy.*

*Daddy.*

*He'd told her.*

Logan shot Rowan a disbelieving look, and he was prepared. He didn't shy away—instead he met her gaze squarely, apparently utterly unrepentant.

She felt completely blindsided and her lips parted to protest, but she swallowed each of the rebukes because this wasn't the time, not in front of Jax.

"We'll talk when Orla arrives," he said casually, as if he hadn't just pulled the ultimate power play, rocking her world again.

How dare he? How dare he?

She was so shocked. So upset. Anger washed over her in hot, unrelenting waves. "Is that what this party was for?"

"Orla will be here in thirty minutes." His voice was calm and quiet but she heard the warning underneath. *Don't do this now. Don't upset Jax.*

She bit back the hot sharp words that filled her head and mouth, battling the sense of betrayal.

He played dirty. He'd always played dirty. He would never change.

Her eyes stung and her throat sealed closed and it was all she could do to hold her emotions in. No wonder he'd been so successful in his career. He was extremely strategic. And he had no conscience. He didn't care who he hurt, not as long as he won.

"You've time for a hot bath and a light bite," he added conversationally. "I'm sure you'd feel better with some coffee and food in you. It's already past lunch. You must be hungry."

"It's past lunch?"

"Yes. It's already after two."

*"Two?"*

"You had a good sleep-in, and a well-deserved one." He briefly turned his attention to Jax as she'd just offered him a little iced cake from her own plate. The cake was now looking a tad sticky but he accepted it with a smile of pleasure.

He held his smile as he focused back on Logan. "I'm glad you slept. I think you were…spent."

She heard his deliberate hesitation and knew exactly what he was implying. She was spent because he'd worn her out with his amazing performance last night.

"It was a grueling day," she agreed shortly, turning away because there was nothing else she could do. She wasn't wanted at the garden party and she was cold in just the T-shirt.

Shivering, Logan returned to the kitchen to see about coffee and one of those scones she'd spotted coming out of the oven.

"Do you think I could get some coffee and one or two of those scones?" she asked the cook.

"I'll send up a tray immediately," the cook promised.

The tray with coffee and scones, and a bowl of fresh berries, was delivered just minutes later to Logan's bedroom, and Logan sat cross-legged on the large bed, enjoying several cups of coffee and the warm flaky scones slathered with sweet Irish butter and an equally thick layer of jam, before bathing and dressing.

By the time Jax returned to the room, Logan was very much ready to shift into mommy mode, but Jax had other ideas. After giving her mother a big hug and kiss she announced that she and Orla were going to watch a movie in the castle theater.

"But wait, how was tea?" Logan asked.

"Lovely."

*Lovely.* Now that wasn't a word American toddlers used often. "Did Orla teach you that word?"

"No, my daddy did."

Once again, *her daddy.*

She ground her teeth together, struggling with another wave of resentment. For the past two plus years she'd been the center of Jax's world, fiercely vigilant, determined to be both mother and father, and yet overnight her role had been changed. She'd been nudged over—no, make that shoved—and she was supposed to be good with it. She was supposed to just accept that Rowan was now in their lives, making changes, shifting power, redefining everything.

"What do you think of him?" she asked carefully.

"My daddy?"

"Yes."

"He's nice."

Logan smiled grimly. "He is, isn't he?"

"Orla says he's lovely."

So that's where she learned the word. Wonderful. "And where is Orla?" Logan asked, determined to hide her anger from Jax, even as she made a mental note of yet one more thing to discuss with Rowan. It was unprofessional for nannies—even cheerful Irish ones—to refer to their male bosses as lovely.

"Outside, in the hall."

Logan went to the door and opened it, and yes, there stood Orla with her ready smile. "Good afternoon," Orla greeted Logan with a lilt in her voice. "Did Jax tell you we're going to go see *Cinderella* in the theater?"

"No." Logan was finding it very difficult to keep up with all the twists and turns in the day. "There's a theater here?"

"Yes, ma'am. Downstairs in the basement."

"Castles have basements?"

"Well, it was the dungeon but we don't want to scare the little girl." And then she winked at Logan. "Or the big girls, either."

And then Orla and Jax were off, walking hand in hand as they headed for the stairs, both apparently very excited about the movie. The movie, undoubtedly, being Rowan's idea.

Which meant it was time to deal with Rowan.

Logan stepped into shoes, grabbed a sweater, and went to find him. It wasn't a simple thing in a castle the size of Ros. She checked the study and then outside, walking through one garden and then another, before returning to the house and climbing the stairs back to the second floor where she opened the door of his bedroom to see if by chance he was there.

He was. And he was in the middle of stripping off his clothes and he turned toward her, completely naked.

Her gaze swept over him, lingering on the thick planes of his chest, the narrow hips, the tight, honed abs and then below. He was gorgeous.

He knew it, too.

"Come back for more, have you?" he asked, his smile cocky.

Logan flushed but didn't run away. She closed the door behind her. "You had no business telling her you were her father—"

"Oh, I absolutely did." His smile was gone. "You were in no hurry to tell her."

"I had a plan."

"I'm sure you did. One that didn't include me." His dark hair was damp. His body still gleamed with perspiration. He made no attempt to cover himself. "But I'm not interested in being shut out or being relegated to the background as if I'm on your staff. I'm her father, not a baby-sitter or hired help."

She wished he'd put his clothes back on. How could she argue with Rowan when he was naked? "I've never said you were hired help," she snapped.

"You certainly haven't treated me as an equal, have you? But you're a Copeland. Why should I expect otherwise?"

"Not that again!"

He walked toward her, muscles taut, jaw tight. "Not that again? I'm not allowed to be troubled by your family? By your sordid history? I'm not supposed to care that your father destroyed my family?" He made a rough low sound, correctly reading her surprise. "Yes. Your father quite handily dismantled my family. It's embarrassing how quickly he ruined us. I blame my father, too. He was the one who chose to work for your father."

He paused to search her face. "Yes, my father once worked for your father. Did you know that?" He laughed shortly, mockingly. "And your father was underhanded even then, already an expert in white-collar crime."

Her heart raced and she held her breath, shoulders squared, bracing herself for the rest.

"Your father has been a sleazy con artist forever. But he was able to get away with it for years, hiding behind his big Greenwich house, with his big Greenwich lifestyle."

Logan swallowed, pulse thudding hard, and yet she refused to say a word, aware that he wasn't done, aware that anything she said would just infuriate him more. The fact that he couldn't accept that she and her father were two different people was his problem, not hers, and it had been his problem from the very beginning. She also understood now that it would never change.

He would never change.

"He was able to hide, your dad, by creating a veneer of

sophistication with money. Other people's money. Taking their incomes and their nest eggs and draining them dry so he could pose and preen, a conscienceless peacock—" He broke off, and looked away, toward the window with the view of the rolling green lawn and the dark hedges beyond.

"There is power in money," he added flatly, harshly after a moment. "It provides an extra layer or two of protection, allowing your father to continue his charade for decades, whereas others, those who worked under him, or for him, were caught up in the schemes and exposed. And those men paid the price early. They went to jail. They served time."

His voice roughened, deepened, and Logan's skin prickled as she suddenly began to understand where Rowan was going with this.

His dad had worked for her father years ago.

Her father had been a con artist even then.

Her father had gotten away with the...schemes...while his father hadn't.

Finally she forced herself to speak. "Your father," she said huskily, "he served time?"

"Yes."

"How long?"

"Long enough." He faced her, expression hard. "It destroyed his reputation, while your father escaped unscathed."

"I don't remember any of this."

"It happened before you were born. I was just a boy, and my brother was a toddler."

She balled her hands into fists, her fingernails digging into her palms. "Why would my father be able to escape unscathed? Why did just your father take the fall?"

"Because my father was paid to take the fall." Rowan's voice was as sharp as glass. "And it wasn't a lot, not even by a poor man's standards, but your father didn't care. It wasn't his problem how the Argyros family survived. It wasn't his problem that a young Irish wife with two young children wouldn't be able to get by when Mr. Argyros went to prison, taking away income. Depriving the family of a father, a husband, a breadwinner."

For a moment there was just silence.

"If your father had been exposed then, if my father had refused to take the fall alone, your father wouldn't have been able to defraud thousands of people billions of dollars. Your father's career as a con artist would have ended. Instead, my father caved and took the blame and served the time, destroying all of us, but leaving you Copelands privileged, spoiled, glamorous and untouched."

And this is why he hated her father so much.

This is why he'd scorned her when he'd discovered who she was.

She was a privileged, spoiled, glamorous, untouched Copeland girl, while he was the son of a man who served time for her father's machinations. "I'm sorry," she whispered, and she really, truly was. She felt the shame of her father's actions so strongly. She'd been deeply ashamed for years, and the weight of the shame had almost suffocated her years ago. It's why she'd moved from the East Coast to the West. It's why she'd pushed her family away. It's why she'd dropped the *Copeland* from her name. Not to hide. She wasn't an ostrich. She'd never buried her head in the sand. She knew how selfish her father was. But it was impossible to survive mired in guilt. The move to California was a desperate, last-ditch effort to shift the pieces in her heart and head so that she could have something of a life. So that she could be someone other than Daniel's daughter.

But Rowan would never see her as anyone but Daniel's daughter.

For Rowan she would always be the enemy.

He shrugged carelessly, callously and turned around, heading for his en suite bathroom. As he walked away from her, she didn't know where to look or what to think or how to feel.

From the back he looked like a Greek god—the very broad shoulders, the long, lean waist, his small tight glutes.

But he also had the cruelty of the Greek gods.

He would punish her forever. He'd never forgive her. She'd spend the rest of her life punished and broken.

Hot tears stung the back of her eyes. "I'm not my father," she shouted after him. "I have never been him, and you are not your father!"

He disappeared into the bathroom. He didn't close the door, but he didn't answer her, either.

"And you have been punishing me from that very first morning in Los Angeles for being a Copeland, and you're still punishing me, and I'm tired of it. I'm tired of this. Your motives aren't pure—"

"No, they're not." He reappeared in the doorway, still stark naked, the hard, carved planes of his body reminding her of the large marble statue of Hercules she'd seen in Rome years ago. "But I take being a parent seriously, as I know how important parents are for young children, and you had no right to cut me out of my daughter's life. I just thank God that your father did die, and I was the one to come for you because otherwise I'd still be oblivious that she even exists."

Fine, he could be livid, but she was seething, too. "I should have been part of that conversation today, Rowan."

"Theoretically, yes, but you weren't there."

"So wait until I am there."

"I'm done waiting," he ground out.

"I should have been there when you told her," she shot

back, walking toward the bathroom. "I should have been part of that conversation."

"Theoretically, yes," he answered, leaning against the door frame, all taut, toned muscle and leashed power. "But there was a moment during our tea when she told me she didn't have a daddy and I was right there, and what was I to do? Pretend I hadn't heard her—"

"She did not say any such thing!"

"She did, *mo ghra*, and so I told her that I was her daddy." He shrugged, straightened. "I didn't make a big deal out of it. I didn't want to overwhelm her. I simply told her I was her father, and I was very sorry to have been away so long, but I wouldn't leave her in the future. I explained that we will all live together now, and we'll be a happy family, the three of us, and hopefully with time, she'd have a baby brother or sister, or both."

Her gaze had been sliding down his body but she jerked it back up, taking in his chiseled jaw, faintly smiling lips, and that impossibly smug expression. "You did not!"

"Oh, I did. And she was excited. She said she'd love a baby brother or sister. Or both. Maybe twins. Twin boys. Twin girls. The more the merrier." He gave her a searching look. "You do want a big family, too, don't you?"

"That's not funny."

"Jax and I are quite serious."

"Don't include Jax in this. She's just a baby herself, which is why you shouldn't lead her on. You'll just disappoint her—"

"But, love, think about it. We didn't use protection last night. You could very well be pregnant already."

She didn't know what to respond to first, his continued use of the word *love* or the suggestion that she could be pregnant. She focused on the second one since they'd both already established that he didn't love. "It takes longer than that for the sperm to travel to the egg," she retorted frostily.

"Maybe I have super sperm." And then flashing her a maddening smile, he turned around, displaying more of his assets, and disappeared into the bathroom.

Logan stood there, fuming, clenching and unclenching her hands. He was so satisfied with himself and so infuriating. And yet, to be fair, she couldn't blame him for feeling victorious. Rowan was proving to be an expert at getting things done, *his way*.

"By the way," Rowan suddenly called to her, even as she heard the shower turn on. "I heard from Drakon earlier today. There seems to be some drama in your family at the moment, and he hoped you could call Morgan after dinner, and I hope so, too, since you've no reason to fight with me—"

"You're trying to pick a fight with me right now."

"I'm trying to get you to focus on the big picture. Your family is in turmoil. You don't need to quarrel with me."

"So just marry you and be done with it. Not want anything for myself. Not need love or kindness."

"I'm very kind to you."

"Rowan!"

"I am. I made you feel so good last night."

"That's not kindness. That's sexual expertise. You're experienced. Technically sound. Big deal."

"It was last night." His voice was somewhat muffled but she still heard the hint of laughter.

"And this is today," she snapped, walking closer to the bathroom. "So what is happening with my family?"

"Your sisters are fighting."

She rolled her eyes. She wasn't surprised. She didn't even need to ask him which sisters. "I warned you that Morgan and Victoria don't get along."

"They seem to have done all right for a day, but then they began discussing the memorial for your father and things fell apart."

"I'm sure I know what happened there. Morgan wants a service and Jemma and Victoria don't, and Morgan's hoping she can convince me to take her side."

"Yes. How did you know?"

She grimaced and rubbed her knuckles over her chin. "It's the story of our family. Even when we try, we can't get along."

"But the news always depicts you four sisters as being very close."

"Lies, all lies," she sang and then her mocking smile slipped. "We've spent our lives being painted as those scandalous Copelands, but we're a family much like anyone else. We have problems. We struggle to agree on things. We have different goals and dreams. But that is far less interesting to the media. I'm afraid we'll always be tabloid fodder."

"Explain the family dynamics to me."

"That would take all day."

"Give me the short version."

"The judge allowed us as children to choose which parent we would live with. We all initially chose to live with Mom, but then Morgan—the most tenderhearted of us—felt sorry for Dad and decided to go live with him, even though he had zero interest in being a father or being there for her. But once she made her decision, she stuck with it, and to this day, she's tried to side with him, which actually just means taking care of him."

"Even though your father stole millions from Drakon?"

She grimaced. "It certainly complicated their marriage, didn't it?"

"So why are Morgan and Victoria so antagonistic? That doesn't make sense to me."

"Morgan wants everyone to forgive Dad, but Victoria isn't sure she can forgive Morgan for siding with Dad. It's endless and exhausting, and between us, I'm tired of it. That's why I moved to California, to get away from the family and the drama."

"Hmm." His deep voice was a rumble from inside the bathroom. "So if Morgan was Team Daniel, and Victoria was his archenemy, where are you on the spectrum?"

She tipped her head, rested it on the door frame. "Probably closer to Victoria, but not as extreme. It's hard because there was Dad and the bitter divorce, and then there was Dad, the investor turned swindler. He made a lot of really bad decisions in his life and now there are five of us trying to move forward, burdened with his...legacy."

Rowan was silent for a bit. "Do you have any good memories of him?"

"Not that I can remember."

"So the memorial service isn't important to you."

"I don't think we need one, but you can't tell Morgan that. She had such a different relationship with him than the rest of us did."

"She's your twin."

"Fraternal. We're nothing alike."

"But weren't you close growing up?"

"Yes. Until she left to go live with Dad." She fell silent a moment, thinking about the complex dynamics. "I do love her, though. She and I have a good relationship. I don't like her being upset."

"According to Drakon she's very upset, but then, so is Victoria."

"And they're still together, under one roof?"

"No, as a matter of fact. Victoria is now on her way

to Jemma's, and based on what I heard from Drakon, you're not going to get your sisters together anytime soon, whether for a memorial service or anything else."

Jemma was married to the powerful King of Saidia, Sheikh Mikael Karim, who'd married her against her will. He was seeking revenge on Daniel Copeland, but by the end of their honeymoon, Jemma and Mikael had fallen in love. He still was not a fan of her father but Mikael was fiercely protective of Jemma. "So they won't be attending our wedding?" Logan said.

The water turned off.

The bathroom was silent except for the drip, drip of water.

Logan grimaced and shook her head. Why did she just say that? What was she thinking? "I was making a joke," she called to him. "Trying to lighten the mood."

He said nothing.

She squirmed, giving herself a mental kick. "That was a joke," she repeated. "We're not getting married. I was trying to be funny."

"I'm sure Drakon and Morgan would come for the wedding," he answered, turning the water back on. "Mikael and Jemma would, too. And probably your mother—"

"Rowan, stop. It was a joke. A bad joke." She peered into the bathroom, unable to see all the way in, but she got a glimpse of the large mirror, clouded with steam. "But speaking of family members. How is Bronson? You haven't said much about him."

"I've been waiting for an update from his doctors." His voice was muffled. The shower sounded louder than before. "There was a setback early this morning."

"A setback?" She waited for him to add more, but he didn't. She took another step into the bathroom. "And? What happened? What's going on?"

"Come all the way in so I don't have to keep shouting."

"I don't want to come in. You're showering."

"I'm sure you've seen a man shower before."

She hesitated. "Actually, I haven't."

For a moment there was just silence and then she heard his low laugh. "Then you *definitely* must come in. Consider it remedial education."

"Not necessary. My education was excellent, thank you. I attended some of the best schools in the world."

He laughed softly again.

# CHAPTER NINE

ROWAN'S WARM, HUSKY LAUGH sent a ripple of pleasure through her, unleashing butterflies in her middle and a rush of warmth in her chest. Why did she respond like that to him? Why did she have to find him so appealing?

He'd simply laughed. That was all. And yet his laugh made her feel good. His laugh didn't just turn her on, it warmed her from the inside out. Damn him.

Logan hovered inside the bathroom doorway and tried to force herself to focus. "How serious is Bronson's setback?" Rowan didn't reply immediately, and she took another tentative step into the warm, humid bathroom. "Is Bronson okay?"

"He's getting the best medical care possible but he's not responding as well as the team hoped." He paused, before asking, "When was the last time you saw him?"

She had to think. "It's been a while. A couple years, maybe. I was pregnant, and then I had Jax, so I wasn't traveling and Bronson is always working. He's spent the past three years working tirelessly to pay back as many of Dad's clients as possible. It's a thankless job, though. Most of the clients are so angry—and yes, they have a right to be, I know—but Bronson didn't steal from them. Bronson had nothing to do with Dad's company, and they don't realize, or maybe they just don't care, that he's sacrificing everything to pay them back."

Water just sluiced down. There was no reply. Not sure if he'd heard her or if he was done talking, she cleared her throat "Why did you ask? Is there something I should know, something you haven't told me?"

Again silence stretched before Rowan said, "He's almost destitute…just one step up from living on the streets."

"No."

"He's been ill, too. He's not in good shape."

"I had no idea. Poor Bronson. So who is with him? Mom?" She found it difficult to reconcile her tall, handsome, successful brother with the one in the hospital. "Are there any leads on who attacked him?"

"Your mother isn't there. She's been fighting something and isn't strong enough to travel."

"So he's alone?"

"Yes, but there is good news. The London police have taken someone in for questioning. It looks like the attack was an isolated incident. Victoria should be able to return home soon."

"That *is* good news."

"So Jax and I could return home soon, too."

"You're free to travel wherever you like."

"Seriously? So I could go to my room and pack right now?"

"Yes."

"You're not worried about losing me?"

"No, because you'd return frequently to see Jax—"

"I'm not leaving Jax here."

"I'm her dad. She needs to be with me."

"I'm her mother, Rowan. She belongs with me."

"Then I guess you might not want to travel for long periods, because this is her home now. And it's your home, too, Logan. That's why we're getting married. We both want Jax to have a family, and stability. There shouldn't be confusion on that." He was silent a moment before adding, "Do you want to come in and give me a hand?"

"A hand doing what?" she asked suspiciously.

"Well, you could wash my back…or something."

She went warm all over, picturing the *something*, and picturing the something growing larger, heavier.

She definitely was curious, and she squirmed a bit, listening to the water stream down, but she didn't like him and didn't trust him, and she hated how he used sex and temptation against her.

"You don't play fair," she called to him, trying not to wonder if he used a lot of soap or body wash, and if he'd lathered himself everywhere. Would he stroke himself as he lathered? Was he stroking himself now? But going down that road…exploring any of those questions would just lead to trouble. He was trouble. Hot, sexy, serious trouble. The trouble that made her drop her guard and lose her reason and she had adorable little Jax as proof. "So, no. Not interested in washing your back. Or anything *else*."

"Should we talk about the wedding then?"

*"Rowan."*

"Jax *is* expecting brothers and sisters."

"Then Jax is going to be disappointed," she answered firmly.

"And what if you are pregnant?"

She really didn't want to think about that. She wasn't pregnant. She couldn't be pregnant.

But he had gotten her pregnant the first time they were together. It could happen again.

"We have to use protection from now on," she said firmly. "We can't take these risks."

"I was thinking we'd get married tomorrow. Jax should be there, of course—"

"No!"

"It's her dream."

"It's also her dream to be a fairy and fly, but that isn't going to happen, either."

"You have no sense of adventure."

He was such a jerk.

Taking a breath for courage, she entered the steamy bathroom. It was a modern bathroom with stylish finishes—marble everywhere, even up to the high ceiling, a huge mirror running the length of a double vanity, and a shower the size of a walk-in closet, the spacious marble shower outfitted with multiple heads to give him an overhead soak as well as a full body spray.

Rowan was standing directly under one of the faucets, dark head tipped back, muscular arm lifted as he ran fingers through his hair, rinsing the shampoo out. His thick biceps was bunched and his flat, hard abdomen was a perfect six pack.

The man was too attractive.

He opened his eyes and looked at her. "You're sure you don't want to wash my…something?" His green eyes glimmered.

*"No."*

"Fine. But do you mind if I do?" he asked pouring body wash into his hand.

Her eyes widened.

Laughing softly he spread the liquid across his chest and then streaked it down his stomach, and then lower to his cock, which was coming to life.

"I did not come in here for a peep show," she said sternly.

"Just trying to get clean, love."

She grimaced, and looked away, not wanting him to know that it was fascinating watching his shaft spring to life and even more fascinating to see how he held it, fisting the length, paying special attention to the thick knob at the end.

And she knew how he was gripping his erection by the reflection in the clear glass shower doors as those hadn't fogged up.

"What's going on with my sister?" she asked, trying to focus on what was important.

"Why didn't you see her for a couple years?" he asked.

From her position she could see his reflection continue to work the soap over his erection. He was slowly, firmly stroking down, working his hand up over the head. Her breath caught in her throat. She squirmed on the inside. "Um," she said, unable to think clearly. "Because I was pregnant…"

"Right." He was stroking down again, the muscles in his forearm cording.

God, he was sexy.

Awful. And sexy. Awfully sexy. Damn him. She dragged in a breath. "So…what's your point?"

"Think about what I'm saying."

"I can't. Not when you're doing…that."

"I knew you were watching." His deep voice was even huskier now than it had been a few moments ago. "Do you want to watch me finish?"

"No!" And then she turned around quickly to look at him. "Are you really going to come?"

His gaze met hers, and one dark eyebrow lifted. "Is that a problem?"

"It just seems…rude…since I'm standing right here."

"You're in my bathroom."

"You invited me in."

"Because you wanted to come in. You were curious. Admit it."

"I wasn't," she protested and then realized he'd stopped handling himself. He still had a huge erection, but he was rinsing off the suds and lather, and then turning off the water.

She glanced uneasily at his erection. "You're just going to leave that, that way?"

"Yes." He leaned out of the shower and grabbed a plush towel from the rack.

"But doesn't it hurt?"

"Not that much."

She couldn't stop looking at him, watching as Rowan dragged the towel over his face, mopping his dark hair and then down his body.

He stopped toweling as he reached his cock. "Sorry. Maybe I'm being dense. Did you want to finish me off?"

"No!" she cried, pretending to be horrified, but then ruined the effect by grinning. "But you should know that that *thing* is very distracting."

He held his arms open, as if giving himself to her.

Logan backed up a step. "I wouldn't even begin to know what to do with it."

"I think you did just fine last night."

"That's because you took the lead on everything."

"I just touched you, love."

That was true. And it had felt wonderful.

She eyed the long, smooth, thick length of him, capped by that equally thick head. She wondered what he'd feel like in her mouth. She wondered what that rounded cap of his would feel like against her lips. She wondered what he'd do if she put her mouth on him.

Pulse quickening, she took a step back toward him. "Can I touch you?"

He nodded, his lashes lowering, hiding his intense green gaze. She was glad. His eyes had a way of seeing too much.

She took another step toward him and, having closed the distance, she put her hands on his chest, his skin so warm beneath her hands, and slid her palms down from his pecs over his ribs to his pelvis with that impressive V-shape.

And then after stealing a peek up into his face—his expression was shuttered and impossible to read—she knelt down in front of him, and dragged her hands down over his hips, along the front of his thighs, his quadriceps rock hard.

His cock bobbed in front of her mouth. She looked at it a little bit warily even as her pulse jumped, adrenaline getting the best of her.

And Rowan, to his credit, just stood there, waiting.

Leaning toward him, she kissed the tip lightly, curious. He was firm, but the skin was soft, warm. She kissed him again, leaving her mouth against him, drinking in his heat and the silky softness as she opened her mouth to touch him with her tongue.

She thought he made a hoarse sound, and she looked up at him, but his expression was blank and so she opened her mouth wider and covered just the tip, and then sucked gently.

He grew even harder as she gently sucked, pulling on him, creating warm wet friction around the head, and then using her tongue to taste and tease the underside of the head.

He made another hoarse sound, and this time she smiled to herself. He didn't hate it. That was something.

Emboldened, she swallowed him even deeper and wrapped what she couldn't take into her mouth with a hand, holding him tightly, and stroking him with her mouth and hand the way she'd seen him touch himself in the shower.

She continued to work him, struggling to get a rhythm

going, but feeling awkward as she ran out of air more than once and needed to pull away so she could get another breath.

He groaned as she broke the rhythm a third time, and she froze, looking up at him apologetically. "I'm sorry. I'm not good at this and you're so big—"

"Don't apologize," he ground out, drawing her to her feet before lifting her up onto the bathroom counter.

He flipped her skirt up and spread her knees wide and then put his mouth on her, over the satin of her panties, and then, pushing the fabric aside, his tongue found her between the slippery folds. She gasped and arched as he flicked her sensitive nib.

"You're already so wet," he said, thrusting a finger into her.

She rocked against his hand, helplessly grinding against him as his sucked on her clit, already close to climaxing. "Sucking on you turned me on," she panted.

"It turned me on, too." His voice was rough, hoarse. "But don't come yet. You have to wait until I tell you."

"I don't think I can—"

He abruptly pulled away and she gasped as he left her. She struggled to pull down her skirt but instead he was taking her off the counter, peeling off her panties and turning her around, bending her over the slab of marble covering the vanity so that her bare butt was exposed.

"Watch me take you," he said. "Watch me fill you. Watch how good we are together."

And then he was parting her legs and running fingers over her, finding her where she was wet. She felt the moment his arousal replaced his fingertips, his thick insistent shaft pressing at her hot core. Her senses spun as he took the thick head and rubbed it up and down her, tak-

ing her creamy heat and spreading it over the tip, making
them both slick.

"Watch," he commanded, putting a hand into her hair
and tugging her head back to see her face in the mirror.
"Watch as I fill you."

And then he was there, entering her, pressing the thick
tip in, stretching her, slowly pushing deeper and deeper.

Her lips parted in a silent gasp of pleasure. He felt so
big, and so hot inside her. It was hard to feel anything but
him buried deep inside her, her body still trying to ac-
commodate his size.

But then Rowan's hands were on her hips, stroking the
outside of her hips and then over the round curve of her
backside, kneading her ass until she wiggled, ready for
more, wanting more.

His hands were under her now, cupping her breasts,
rubbing the nipples, making her gasp.

"Look at you," he growled. "You're so beautiful."

"No."

"You are, and you're mine. We belong together, *mo
ghra*. Can't you see that?"

She didn't know where to look. She was pressed close
to the mirror, and she felt so much that it was hard to take
in what she was seeing. Instead she got impressions—her
pink cheeks, her bright eyes, her lips parted and swollen,
while behind her Rowan was all hard, taut muscle. He
looked powerful and primal and...happy.

It crossed her mind that he might just like her.

That he might truly want her.

She exhaled in a rush as he rubbed her sensitive nipples, kneading them, making her hotter, wetter, making
her tighten convulsively around him.

"Keep watching." His deep voice was practically purr-
ing. "Watch us."

Her breath hitched as he slid a hand from her breasts, down over her belly, to settle between her thighs, and then hitched again as he parted her curls and the soft inner lips to stroke her swollen clit.

He played her clit without moving his hips and it wasn't fair—to feel so much fullness within her while he teased all those nerve endings—she wouldn't be able to resist him long.

"I'm going to come," she said breathlessly. "I can't stop it this time."

"Yes, you can."

"No, I can't."

And just like that his hand fell away, and he pulled out of her, and she nearly screamed with frustration at the deep intense ache within her that was part emptiness and part pain. Tears started to her eyes and turning around she beat him on his chest. "I hate you for doing that. Why do that?"

"Because when you delay an orgasm, it makes it even stronger when you do finally come—"

"I don't *want* it to be even stronger. I just want you." She beat one more time on his chest, this time for emphasis. "So stop messing around. Give me you." Her hands reached for his neck and she pulled his head down to her and she kissed him desperately. "I want you, you awful horrible addictive man." And then she was kissing him again, kissing him as if her life depended on it.

The kiss felt different.

Rowan had kissed Logan before. He'd kissed countless women before. But there had never been a kiss quite like this one.

It was hot and fierce and edged with a hunger that stirred his blood, but there was something else in it, too. Something…open. Something vulnerable.

Not that she was giving herself to him, but instead asking for something of him. And it wasn't a sexual commitment. It was bigger than that. Deeper.

She wanted *him*.

As his hands rose to clasp her face, his palms cradling her jaw so that he could kiss her more deeply, it struck him that she was looking for truth. She was looking for safety. She was looking for someone who would accept her, offering herself in return.

She'd been like this that first night together, the night of the auction…fierce, intense, warm, open.

He hadn't known her then. He hadn't realized she was a virgin. Hadn't understood that she hadn't merely been offering her body, but she'd been giving him her heart.

He understood it now. He understood her.

And this time, he wasn't throwing her gift away.

Rowan scooped her up in his arms and carried her through the bathroom to the bedroom where he placed her on the bed.

He stretched out over her, and she parted her knees for him, making room for him.

"I won't stop this time," he murmured. "And I'm not going away. I'm going to make you feel good, and I'm going to keep making you feel good until you and I are finally on the same page."

"That's going to take a lot of sex."

"Good thing we both like it."

He positioned himself between her thighs, finding her where she was so soft and wet and ready for him. He heard her sigh as he slid in, felt her hips tilt to welcome him. He nearly growled with pleasure as she accepted him, taking him deep. She was tight and hot and her body clenched him, holding him.

He loved being buried within her. Everything felt right

when he was with her like this, and everything would be perfect if he knew he hadn't hurt her.

But he had.

And he couldn't go back, and he couldn't change his reaction that morning in her kitchen, and he couldn't change the fact that he'd scorned her when she phoned weeks later, but he could give himself to her now. He could be real with her now.

He pressed up, resting his weight on his forearms, then he slowly drew out of her before burying himself deep again. He kissed her as his hips thrust, his tongue probing her mouth, stroking to match the friction of his shaft.

It felt so good being with her. He felt so good with her. He didn't want the pleasure to end. This was sex, but not merely sex, it was more. He couldn't explain it, and didn't want to try. He just knew that he'd taken so many women to bed, and no one had ever felt like Logan. No one had ever made him feel the way Logan did. With her, he felt settled. Calm. Whole.

Logan was trembling. She was so close…so close to coming but she couldn't come. The two almost times in the bathroom had made it impossible to go over the edge. Instead she was restless and aching, everything inside her wound so tight that she couldn't stop her legs and body from trembling.

Rowan's mouth covered hers and his large, powerful body rode hers, but she felt almost frantic as the orgasm remained out of reach.

Her hands slid down his back to cling to his hips. She flexed her fingers against his firm butt, his skin so warm, his body creating friction everywhere—his chest against her breasts, his cock inside of her. And yet the friction was just that, delicious sensation, but she couldn't reach the point that would give her relief.

She whimpered, muscles tight, need flooding her. She closed her eyes, trying to concentrate to see if she could find relief, but his hard heat inside of her wouldn't push her to that pinnacle.

"Rowan," she pleaded, gripping his hips. "Rowan... I can't..."

"You can." And then he slipped his hand between them, finding her sensitive nub and one, two and the sensation focused and narrowed, tension building, tightening, until there was no turning back.

She shattered, and kept shattering, the orgasm going on and on as if it would never end.

In a distant part of her brain she registered Rowan's deep groan, and his hard thrust, reaching release, before holding still, and just holding her.

She didn't know how long they lay there, warm and spent. She was truly spent, too. Her eyes closed. She exhaled and was soon fast asleep.

Logan didn't know how much time had passed when she finally opened her eyes because the room was swathed in shadows but it wasn't completely dark outside. She must have slept a good couple of hours though because she'd been dreaming until just a few moments ago, and the dream was good. She woke up feeling happy.

Stretching slightly she shifted, and became aware of Rowan's arm wrapped around her waist. She turned to look at him. He was awake and watching her. "Do you know what time it is?" she asked, her voice rough with sleep.

"Almost time to get up," he answered, kissing her forehead. "We're having dinner with Jax soon."

"We are?"

"Yes."

"You make it all sound so normal. As if we're a real family."

"We are a real family, and it is our new normal," he answered quietly, but there was no smile in his voice or eyes. His expression was somber. Even his green eyes looked dark.

*We are a real family... And this is our new normal.*

"We don't feel like a family," she said carefully, after a moment.

"Not yet maybe. But we will, with time."

She stared into his eyes, wishing she could see past the beautiful dark green color, wishing she could see him. "I know nothing about you, you know. We've only had sex."

"And a child."

"But it's really just been sex—"

"We did talk about your family earlier. It could almost be considered a real and meaningful conversation."

She felt like punching him in the chest again. "So tell me about your family. Open up about your world. Have a *meaningful* conversation with me."

"To be honest, I'd prefer to make you come again."

"Yes, I'm sure you would."

"Sex isn't a bad thing," he answered mildly, reaching out to stroke the swell of her breast and the firming nipple. "Sex creates life, and intimacy—"

"So does conversation, and sharing. And it's your turn to share. Tell me more about your family. Where are your parents now? What happened to your father after he served time? Do you see either of them often? And why did you go into the military? What was its appeal?"

He rolled onto his back and drew her with him so that she lay on top of his chest. "I'd rather not talk about boring things when we can talk about us. Did you like seeing us together in the mirror? How did it make you feel to watch me take you?"

"We're not discussing sex!" She shoved up, pushing away from his chest. "And you have to tell me something about you. I can't keep sleeping with a complete enigma!"

"You can if you like him."

"I don't particularly like him." She glared down at him, frustrated and yet aware that he was really handsome, and really appealing, and she could maybe see a future with him, but not as a married couple...rather, as lovers. Lovers that coparented. Or something of that nature. "And you have to share relevant things that I want to know. Otherwise, we can't keep doing this."

"Now you're just punishing yourself. We both know you like doing what we do."

She gave him a thump on his chest. "What were your parents' names?"

He sighed. "Darius and Maire. He was Greek American and she was Irish American, but neither lived long in the US. My mother was from this area, and my father from Rhodes, Greece, and they both had strong accents, hers Irish, his Greek. They drank hard, they loved hard, they fought hard, and they seemed determined to make it work, even when Dad went to prison, but when my little brother died, the love died, leaving just hard drinking and lots of fighting."

She closed her eyes and rested her head on his chest. "Do you remember Devlin?"

"Yes."

"What was he like?"

"Sweet. Happy." He paused, drew a breath. "Devlin was a truly happy little boy. He was always smiling. He had a huge laugh." His voice deepened, roughened. "I remember I used to love to carry him because he smelled good. He still had that baby smell."

Logan blinked back tears. "You must have taken his death so hard."

Rowan didn't answer but she felt the tension within him.

After a moment he said quietly, "Jax looks a lot like him. It's a bit disconcerting. If I could find a picture of Devlin I'd show you."

"I believe you."

He smoothed her hair. "What else?" he asked after a moment. "What are you aching to know?"

She smiled at his choice of words. "Do you like having dual citizenship?"

"I had three passports at one point—Greek, Irish and American, but I tried not to travel with three. It's confusing for border agents."

The corner of her mouth curled higher. "And your parents? Are either of them still alive?"

He hesitated. "Dad died of lung cancer a couple years ago, and she has dementia but I go see her every week or so when I'm here."

"She still lives near here?"

"Yes, she's in a care facility just down the road."

"You didn't want her here?"

"She was here until six months ago when she escaped her minder and tumbled down the stairs." He was no longer smiling. He looked tense and grim. "Her new home is top-notch and provides excellent care."

"I'm not judging."

He exhaled slowly. "No one wants to put their mother in a home. It doesn't feel natural."

Logan said nothing, sensing that he wasn't done, and she didn't want to stop him from saying more.

After a moment he shrugged. "I'd like to take Jax to

meet her. You can come, too. But Mother rarely recognizes me these days. She thinks I'm that nice man who plays the piano for dancing."

"Do you play the piano?"

"No. But she and my father met at a party and there was dancing, so maybe she thinks I'm my father." His brow furrowed. "Or the piano player."

Logan leaned up and kissed him. "They both sound like nice people," she whispered, kissing him again. "And I think it's a lovely idea to take Jax to see your mother."

They ended up making love again and it was different than it had been so far, sweeter and calmer but emotionally more intense.

Logan felt connected to Rowan in a way she hadn't felt before.

Maybe it's because she'd had a glimpse behind the mask. She was grateful he'd shared with her, even though it was clear he didn't like sharing. She was also touched that he'd tried to keep his mother with him, at Castle Ros, and that it had been a struggle putting her in a care facility.

Clearly he wasn't all bad.

Clearly he was rather good…maybe even very good…

She held her breath, scared to admit to everything she was feeling. It was confusing and overwhelming. So much was happening but she wasn't sure if any of this was right. She didn't want to go through life on her own, a single mother forever, but at the same time, sharing Jax would mean relinquishing control.

It would mean trusting Rowan to do the right thing.

It would mean trusting that she would do the right thing.

It would mean compromising and yielding and sacrificing independence, too.

Could she do that? Did she even want to do that?

Which brought her back around to the issue of control.

Control was such a huge thing for her because the loss of control always resulted in loss. As soon as she lost control, bad things happened. Without control she wouldn't be able to protect herself, never mind Jax.

Panic building, Logan rolled away from Rowan. "Time to get dressed," she said, rolling off the bed and heading for the bathroom.

She was quickly gathering her clothes when Rowan followed her in. "I feel like you're running away," he said, blocking the doorway. "Why?"

"Not running away. It's just getting late, and I need to shower and dress for dinner," she answered, unable to look at him.

"Everything was fine and now you're shutting down again—"

"I'm not shutting down!" she snapped, shooting him a fierce look. "And I'm certainly not running away, either. How can I run when you've brought me to your high-tech castle with bodyguards and security cameras and massive hedges everywhere?" Her voice cracked. "Look at me, Rowan! I'm naked in your bathroom with you blocking the doorway. I'm trapped."

"You're not trapped," he retorted impatiently, moving toward her.

She retreated, moving away until she bumped into the thick glass shower enclosure. "No? Then what do you call this..." she gestured wildly at the shrinking space between them because he was coming toward her again, rapidly closing the distance. "You're everywhere and you're overwhelming and overpowering, and I can't breathe or think or feel when you're with me—" She broke off as he pressed himself against her, his knee between her legs, his hands capturing hers, pinning them to the glass above her head. "See?" she choked as his fingers entwined hers and his head dipped, his mouth on her neck, setting her skin on fire. "You're doing it again…confusing me…overpowering me…making it impossible to think."

"What do you need to think about, *mo chroi*?" he murmured, kissing higher, just beneath her earlobe. "And why do you need to fight me? We work, you and I. We fit."

She shuddered against him, her breasts firming, nipples tightening as heat flooded her. She ached on the inside again, ached for him again. She loved the feel of him, loved it when he was in her, making her body feel so good, but he had the opposite effect on her head and heart.

He wasn't good for her. He wasn't right for her. He wasn't what she wanted—

*No, not true.*

She wanted him, but that didn't make it right. She needed a man who allowed her to be calm. She needed a man who made her feel safe—not safe in terms of keeping the bad guys of the world away, but safe emotionally. Safe as in loved.

He touched her and created energy and passion and excitement, but it was all so wild and dangerous.

And then he was kissing her, his lips on hers and there was so much heat and hunger that all the wild, chaotic emotion rushing through her slowed, thickened, turning to honey and wine in her veins.

He made her feel so much…

He made her want so much…

He made her want everything…and that included love. The more he touched her, the more pleasure he gave her, the more she wanted love.

His love.

Tears burned the back of her eyes, and her chest squeezed tight, her heart turning over. Making love made her want his love, and he was the first to admit he didn't love. No, he just offered sex. Lots and lots of hot sex, but sex without love was empty, and it would hollow her out, leaving her empty.

"Your idea of a happy relationship is sex," she answered, her voice faint. "But my idea of a happy relationship is love. Do you love me? Can you love me? Can you answer that?"

"When I touch you, do I make you feel good? When I hold you, do you feel desirable?"

"I want love and you want sex!"

"I want you, and I feel close to you through sex." He swore, and he rarely swore. "Hell, I am close to you during sex. I'm in you, love. We're as close as two people can be."

She didn't know how to respond to that.

"Sex can be a lot of things," he added. "Tender, rough, sweet, aggressive. It changes, just as we change, but sex creates a bond, creating something we only have together."

"But that's the problem. I don't want to bond through sex. I want love because love is the ultimate bond. It is the thing that keeps people committed when desire fades or someone is ill. If all we have is sex, what happens when sex isn't available? Does the relationship end? Are we done? What will keep us together?"

"Jax," he said promptly. "She'll keep us together."

She made a rough sound. "And what if something happens to her?" He said nothing and she searched his eyes, and she had the answer there.

Nothing would keep them together. Their relationship would end and the time they spent together would have meant nothing.

Logan shook her head. "This is why I keep repeating myself—I'm not settling. I'm not getting married for sex. If I marry, it will be because I've made a commitment for life to a man. That's the only reason to marry. Because I want to be with him. Forever."

His hands fell away. He stepped back.

She swallowed the lump in her throat. "Can I please dress now?"

He let her dress and go.

# CHAPTER TEN

THEY HAD DINNER with Jax in the castle's "small" dining room, a room that still featured massive wooden beams and a huge iron chandelier and tapestries on two walls depicting a violent medieval battle, not to mention two suits of armor.

Jax was fascinated by the armor and the stone fireplace and the tapestry with the violent battles. She was the one to point out that even the intricate carvings worked into the mantel were of "fighting."

"Ireland is a very old country," Rowan explained to her. "It has a long history, and fortunately, or unfortunately, there have been many battles fought here."

Jax turned her wide blue eyes on him, studying him now with intense interest. "Fighting is bad."

"Fighting isn't good, no," he answered, "but sometimes you fight to protect things…your country, your family, your home."

She digested this in silence and then just moments later, slid out of her chair again to go study the fireplace once more.

In the end, there was very little real eating done, and mostly explanations and exploration, but Logan didn't mind. She'd found it difficult to eat tonight, her emotions still raw, her thoughts painfully convoluted.

And Jax was even doing her a favor, providing a diversion, keeping Rowan occupied with all her questions about war and Ireland and the coats of armor at both sides of the room, keeping Logan and Rowan from speaking to each other very much.

But finally, after dessert had been served, Orla appeared and offered to give Jax a bath and read her a story, promising Logan and Rowan that she'd let them know when Jax was ready to sleep, so they could come up and kiss her good-night.

Rowan glanced at Logan as if to let her decide.

Logan looked at her daughter who was already talking animatedly to Orla and seemed more than happy to leave the dining room and return upstairs.

Logan nodded consent, unable to argue with the plan, while at the same time aware that once Jax was gone, she and Rowan would be left alone together and they'd have to address the uncomfortable tension that had hummed in the dining room since the beginning of the meal.

"What do you want?" he asked her, breaking the silence. "What will make this better? What else can I tell you about my family, or my past, to show you who I am and help you believe that I'm committed to you—to us—and that I think we can be happy without all the hearts and fuss and romance."

"I'm not asking for hearts and fuss," she answered. "And you mock me when you imply that my needs are so trivial."

"I'm not trying to mock you, or trivialize what you feel. If anything I'm frustrated that you don't understand that what we do have is good. What we have physically is explosive and intense and deeply satisfying, and it's not often like this. To be honest, I've never known this with any other woman. I've only ever found this with you."

She froze, not certain what to do with that. She searched his face, scrutinizing his hard, masculine features, wishing she could believe him.

Would he lie to her?

Her brow creased, as she struggled to remember if he'd ever lied to her. He'd been harsh…cruel…but she didn't think he'd ever lied before, which was key. She hated liars. Hated to be played…

Her father had played them. Her father had turned them all into fools.

"But maybe I'm wrong," he added after a moment. "Maybe you've found this…connection…with someone else. Maybe there was someone who made you feel better."

"I've never been with anyone but you, so I wouldn't know," she answered flatly.

She saw the moment her words registered.

"You've only *ever* been with me?" he asked.

Her shoulders twisted. She kept her voice cool. "The night in California and then here."

He exhaled slowly, his forehead furrowed, expression troubled. "So you really don't know about… You have nothing to measure this—us—by."

She didn't know what he meant by that or how to answer something like that, and so she didn't.

Thank God he didn't ask why, because that would mean he truly didn't understand how difficult the past few years had been. That would mean he still believed she was that spoiled, pampered, selfish Copeland girl…

But he didn't ask why and she didn't have to defend herself. She didn't have to throw in his face that society continued to ostracize her and her siblings, making it almost impossible for them to make a living.

No, life had not been easy, and especially for her, once

pregnant, it became downright brutal. There had been no time for men. There had been no time for herself.

And even if there had been time to date…she wouldn't have. She didn't want another man. She'd wanted him. She'd fallen for *him*. Which, in many ways, was the greatest shame of all.

"We can make this work," Rowan said abruptly, leaving his chair, and walking toward her. "We can give Jax something better than what I knew and better than what I had. I want her to have stability and laughter and fun and adventure, and that can happen, but you and I, we have to get along."

"Isn't that what we're doing now? Trying to figure out how we can make this work?"

"I'm not sure anymore. I worry that you've already decided that it won't work, and you're just placating me until you can leave." He stopped in front of her, expression brooding. "But if you leave, it means Jax won't ever have one home. She'll end up like me, bouncing back and forth between homes and countries…different cultures, different customs, different schools. It's a lonely life for a child—"

"As well as a lonely life for me. Do you think I want my daughter living halfway around the world without me? Do you think I want to miss Christmas with her or a birthday celebration?" She was on her feet, too, her dinner chair between them, because God help her, he couldn't touch her again. She couldn't let him close because every time he reached for her, she melted, but giving in to him only made things worse. It made her hate him despite herself. "I don't want to live without my daughter. But I won't be forced into living with you, either!"

"I'm not forcing you. I want you to want to be here—"

"But I don't want to be here. I didn't choose to be here. And I didn't choose *you*."

"You did once."

She flushed, remembering the auction and how she'd put herself into a terrible financial situation just to be with him.

Even then, she was weak.

Even then, she was a fool.

"Yes, you're right," she whispered, heartsick all over again. "I did choose you and then you crushed me. Like a bug under the heel of your shoe." She gulped air, arms folding tightly across her chest to keep from throwing up. "And I'm just supposed to forget about what you did, right? I'm just supposed to act like it didn't happen. Well, it did happen! And it *hurt*. You almost broke me, Rowan. You made me question my own sanity and I'm not interested in ever feeling that way again."

She drew deep rough breaths as she backed away from him. "For one night I was yours, Rowan. All yours. And then I discovered what it means to be yours. And I have no desire, ever, to be yours again."

She started for the door, walking quickly to escape the room as fast as possible, but his voice stopped her midway.

"Forgive me, Logan," he said quietly. "Please."

For a long moment there was just silence. She couldn't bring herself to answer, and she wouldn't let herself look at him, either.

Finally when the silence had become suffocating and her body quivered with tension, she shook her head, and without a glance back, walked out.

But once at the stairs, Logan choked on a smothered cry, and dashed up the steep steps, taking them two at a time, trying to escape the hot, livid pain streaking through her heart.

Jax was asleep when Logan reached the room, and after saying good-night to Orla, Logan changed into her pajamas, but she couldn't get into bed—she was too wound up.

She paced until she couldn't take another step, and then she finally sank onto the plush rose-and-ruby carpet in front of the fireplace, and closed her eyes, trying to clear her head and get some much needed calm and perspective.

But every time she drew a deep breath, she felt a sharp ache in her chest and it hurt so much that she couldn't focus.

He'd asked her to forgive him, and she'd refused. *Refused*.

That was horrible. She felt horrible, but if she forgave him, truly forgave him, then she'd have no way to resist him, because she already cared too much for him. She was already far too invested.

Her anger was all she had left to try to protect herself. Without her anger she'd have no armor, and without armor, he could break her all over again.

But hanging on to the anger would destroy her, too. Anger was so toxic. It was poison for the soul.

She didn't want to be angry with him, but she also didn't want to stay here and give up the last of her dreams. She wanted a family for Jax, but she also wanted love for herself and it wasn't enough to be Rowan's sex kitten.

As much as she enjoyed being in his bed, she wanted his heart more than his body.

It was time to leave.

She'd pack tonight and leave tomorrow. Rowan would have to let her go. She rose and went to pull her suitcase out from beneath her large canopy bed but was stopped by a knock on her bedroom door.

It was Rowan, she was sure of it. She could feel his very

real, very physical energy on the other side of the door and her pulse quickened in response, her heart beating faster.

She retrieved the suitcase, placing it at the foot of the bed, and then went to open the door.


Rowan was not a masochist, and he was not looking forward to another conversation with Logan tonight. The last one had been more than sufficient for a single evening. But he'd promised to let her know if there was news regarding her brother, and there was news. And it wasn't good.

Logan opened the door. She was wearing red and pink plaid pajama pants and a pink knit top that hugged her breasts, making it clear she wasn't wearing a bra. But there was no smile as she looked at him, her jaw set, her eyes shadowed.

"Hope you weren't asleep," he said gruffly.

"No." Her lips compressed and her chin lifted. "I don't want to do this with you, Rowan. I don't want to keep fighting—"

"Bronson's not doing well," he interrupted quietly. He gave her a moment to let his words sink in. "His body seems to be shutting down."

She blinked, and looked at him, clearly confused.

He hated this next part and drew a swift breath. "They suggested it might soon be time to think about saying goodbye."

*"What?"*

"Are you comfortable leaving Jax with Orla? We could fly to London first thing tomorrow and be at the hospital by nine?"

"No. *No.* He's only in his midthirties. How can his body be shutting down?"

"He wasn't strong before he was shot and he's not responding well to treatment."

Logan struggled to speak but the words wouldn't come. She looked away, eyes gritty, throat sealing closed. "Why isn't he responding to treatment?"

"He'd been ill for weeks before he was shot. His body just can't keep fighting."

"I want to go to him now."

"They have him sedated. You won't be able to see him until tomorrow."

"I want to be there when he wakes up."

"You will be. We'll go in the morning—"

"I'll go in the morning," she corrected. "Jax and I will go. This is a Copeland family matter, and you hate the Copelands."

"You can't take Jax to the hospital."

"We're going, Rowan." She stepped aside and gestured to the suitcase by the bed. "I'd already planned on leaving. You just need to put us on a plane and get us to London so I can see my brother. He needs me."

He heard the words she didn't say. Bronson needed her, whereas he, Rowan Argyros, didn't. "And what about Jax?" he said gruffly.

Her eyes suddenly shone with tears. "You'll miss her, but not me," she said with a rough, raw laugh before shaking her head. "Don't worry. I won't keep her from you. I promise to sort out custody and visitation rights, but surely we can do it later, when my brother isn't dying?"

Rowan's chest squeezed. He felt an odd ache in his chest. And looking at her in the doorway, in her pink-and-red pajamas, wearing no makeup, her long hair in a loose ponytail, she looked young and impossibly pretty, and it crossed his mind that one day Jax would look just like this: fresh, sweet, pretty. Little girls did grow up. Little girls became grown-up girls and grown-up girls should never be crushed. Not by anyone.

"We can make this work, Logan. You just have to give us a chance."

She made a soft, rough sound and blinked away tears. "I did. And the sex was great. It was fantastic. But I don't want your body, Rowan, not without your heart."

# CHAPTER ELEVEN

THE FLIGHT TO LONDON was short, just an hour and fifteen minutes long. Rowan had let them go, putting them on his plane first thing in the morning. But he hadn't sent them off alone. He'd sent Orla with them as well as passports, including a brand-new Irish passport for Jax.

She had no idea how he'd managed that feat. But then, he had incredible connections, having worked for several governments.

Logan looked from Jax's new passport to Jax where the little girl sat quietly in Orla's arms across from her, and then to Orla herself and suddenly something about the Irish nanny made Logan stare harder.

Orla looked less like an Irish nanny this morning and more like…

Protection.

Logan frowned slightly, brows pulling.

Orla must have read Logan's expression because she suddenly asked Logan, "Are you okay, Miss Copeland?"

Logan nodded once, but she wasn't really okay. Her heart hurt. And she was worried about Bronson. And she couldn't see the future. And she wasn't even sure the nanny was a real nanny anymore…

"Orla, are you really a professional nanny?" Logan

asked, feeling foolish for voicing the question but unable to stop herself.

"I did go to nanny college, and I have worked for quite a few years now as a nanny. Why do you ask?"

"Because you remind me a little bit of Joe."

Orla's eyebrows arched.

"Joe was my assistant in Los Angeles," Logan added. "Or I thought he was my assistant. It turned out he was a former member of an elite military group and an employee of Dunamas. And I just wondered if maybe you were also Dunamas."

Orla just looked at her.

"Because I don't see Rowan letting us leave Ireland without security. I can't help thinking that maybe you're… security."

Orla's lips curved, her expression amused. "You know Mr. Argyros well."

Castle Ros felt empty without Logan and Jax. Rowan felt empty without Logan and Jax. He missed them already and they'd only been gone four hours.

He paced his study and then the library and then the length of the castle and finally the gardens, ignoring the drizzly rain.

He shouldn't have let them go. It was a mistake to let them go. And he'd been the one to put them on the jet this morning. He'd personally escorted them onto the plane, checking seat belts, trying to do whatever he could to keep his family safe.

He'd come so close to telling Logan that he'd changed his mind, that they couldn't go. Or at least, they couldn't go without him. But she'd refused to look at him, refused to speak, other than to murmur a quiet, taut thanks.

And then he'd walked off the plane and the crew shut

the door and the jet raced down the runway, before lifting off.

He felt as if his heart had gone with them, which was so odd as he didn't have a heart. He was, as Logan mocked, worse than the Tin Man…

But she was wrong. He had a heart and he did care. He just didn't know how to prove it to her since he didn't trust words. He'd never liked them. Actions always spoke louder.

Actions, not words.

Once on the ground, they transferred into a waiting car. It was raining and the city streets were crowded but the driver navigated the traffic with ease, getting them to the private hospital in less time than the driver had anticipated.

Logan, who had been calm until now, was nervous, her stomach doing uncomfortable flips. She leaned down to kiss the top of Jax's head, trying not to let her anxiety get the best of her. Bronson had to be okay. Bronson was the most ethical, moral man she knew. He'd spent the last three years trying to pay every investor back, working tirelessly to make amends.

She looked up and her gaze met Orla's. Orla's expression was sympathetic.

"I'm scared," Logan confessed.

"It'll be all right, now that you're here," Orla answered firmly.

"You think so?"

"Everyone needs family. He'll do better now that you're at his side."

Logan nodded and exhaled, forcing a smile. "So what are you and Jax going to do while I'm with Bronson? Go straight to the hotel or…?"

"I think we will go check in and maybe have a snack

and perhaps a nap. Don't worry about us. Focus on your brother."

She nodded again, hands clenched as she glanced out the window at the streets of London, but she couldn't focus on the city, not when she kept thinking about Bronson, and then Rowan.

Rowan who'd let them go.

Rowan who'd stopped fighting her and given in.

Funny how he finally gave her what she wanted, but she felt no relief. She felt just pain.

Just waves of sorrow, of deep aching grief.

The driver slowed before the hospital and then parked beneath the covered entrance and came round the side of the car to open the passenger door.

Logan kissed Jax goodbye and then stepped from the car, squaring her shoulders as she faced the hospital's front door.

There were several rounds of desks and locked doors to pass through, some of the locked doors security to protect Bronson from outsiders, while the last was the hospital's intensive care unit, where they were fighting to keep Bronson alive.

After checking in at the desk in ICU, she went to Bronson's room. She stopped in the doorway and struggled to process everything. The hospital equipment. The monitors. The patient in the bed.

Tears filled her eyes. She drew a quick fierce breath, and then entered, going straight to the side of the bed, where she leaned over Bronson and carefully, tenderly kissed his cheek.

For the next four hours Logan sat next to Bronson's bed. He slept the entire time she was there. The doctors and nurses came and went, checking the monitors, changing IV bags to keep him hydrated, shifting the bed a little to raise his head to ease his breathing.

She felt so guilty as she sat there next to him. He'd spent the past three years fighting to repay debts that were not even his. He'd battled alone, determined to clear the Copeland name.

It was an unbearable burden.

A thankless job.

And he'd never once complained.

Blinking away tears, she reached for his hand again. He needed to be okay. He needed to recover and have a life that mattered, because he mattered. But it wasn't easy keeping vigil. He wasn't the brother she remembered.

Bronson was handsome, heartbreakingly handsome, and yet he'd never paid the slightest bit of attention to his looks. He wasn't shallow or superficial. He had heart. And integrity. So much integrity. He was nothing like their father...

"Hey, Lo," a rough voice rasped.

She sat up quickly and moved closer to him. *"Bronson."*

His blue gaze met hers. He struggled to smile. "What brings you to London?"

"You." She leaned down, kissed his forehead and then murmured, "Oh, Bronson, what's happened to you?"

"Doesn't matter. I'm just glad to see you. I've missed you."

Tears filled her eyes and she couldn't stop them. "I've missed you, too, and I'm so sorry I wasn't here before."

"You're here now," he rasped, before closing his eyes again.

Bronson slept for another three hours and Logan just sat next to him, unable to imagine leaving him here alone.

She was grateful she didn't need to worry about Jax. Grateful that Orla was there. Grateful that Rowan had sent Orla. Grateful that Rowan wouldn't let anything happen to Jax...or her.

Bronson woke up again just before dinner. He seemed

pleased, even relieved, to see that Logan was still there. "Still here, Lo?"

She smiled at him. "Where else would I be?"

"Home, taking care of your baby."

"She's not much of a baby anymore. Jax is two, and she's here in London right now, not California."

"I'd love to meet her. I'm sorry I haven't been out your way—"

"We've all been busy. It's not been easy. I know." She reached for his hand and gave it a squeeze. "Bronson, I need you to get better. And I'm going to do whatever I have to do to make sure you have the right care...the best care—"

"I am getting it," he rasped, gesturing up toward the equipment. "I couldn't get better care than this, and it's because of you."

"Not me."

"Yes, you. Your friend Rowan did this. Arranged this. I'm alive because of him."

*Her friend Rowan.*

Her eyes burned and her throat sealed closed. She gripped his hand tighter. "He's not my friend." Her voice was hoarse and unsteady. "But he is the father of my daughter."

Bronson's gaze met hers. "Why isn't he your friend?"

"He's not. He's never been my friend."

"Then why would he do all this? Get me this help? Fly you here?"

"How did you know he flew me here?"

"Well, you're here, and he's here, so..." His voice faded as his gaze lifted, his attention focused on the door.

Logan turned around, glancing toward the door, and yes, there was Rowan, on the other side of the observation glass.

Her heart thudded extra hard. She had to blink to clear her eyes.

"Jax's father," Bronson said even more faintly, clearly tired.

"Yes." She turned back to her brother. His eyes were closed. "Sleep," she murmured, giving his hand a squeeze. "I'll be here when you wake."

Logan left Bronson's side and stepped out of his room into the hall. Rowan was no longer outside Bronson's room but heading for the elevator.

She raced after him, catching him before he could take the elevator down. "What are you doing? Where are you going?" she demanded breathlessly.

"I left some things for you. Some snacks, a toothbrush, a change of clothes. Knowing you, you're not going to want to leave him tonight."

Her chest squeezed, making her heart ache. She searched his face, trying to see what he was thinking or feeling but Rowan was so damn hard to read, never mind reach. "But why were you leaving without speaking to me?"

His powerful shoulders shifted. "I think everything has been said already."

Her eyes burned and frustration washed through her, hot and fierce. Not true, she thought. He hadn't yet said the things she needed to hear.

She saw him look past her, down toward her brother's room. "How is he?" Rowan asked.

"Weak, but mentally clear." She swallowed. "He said you arranged for his care. That he's here in this hospital because of you."

Rowan shrugged carelessly.

Logan struggled to find the right words. "He thinks

you're my friend. I had to correct him. Because we're not friends. We've never been friends."

He just looked at her, eyes bright but hard. Just like the rest of him.

She pressed on, emotion thickening her voice. "We were lovers and then enemies. And now parents."

"What do you want me to say?" he demanded tautly.

She was silent a moment, thinking. "I just want to understand."

"Understand what?"

"What would have happened that morning if we'd had coffee and breakfast in my kitchen, and you'd glanced at the magazine and my name had simply been Logan Lane... what would have happened with us if I hadn't been Logan Lane Copeland?"

He didn't take long to answer. "I would have married you," he said flatly.

She went hot then cold. It was the last thing she'd expected him to say.

His green gaze darkened. "You weren't just sex. You were never just sex. You were home."

She couldn't breathe. She couldn't think. She just stared at him, numb.

"I'd never felt that way with anyone before," he added curtly. "And I doubt I'll ever feel that way again." His strong jaw tightened. "I've only ever wanted you. And I still only want you."

*I still only want you.*

"Because the sex was so good?" she whispered.

"Because you were so good. You were...are...the other half of me."

Her eyes burned and she didn't know where to look or what to say. If that wasn't a declaration of love, she didn't know what was, and yet she'd told him so many times that she wanted love. She wanted to be loved. And it suddenly crossed her mind that maybe they were just using different words for the same thing. *"Rowan."*

But he took a step back, putting space between them, and pushed the elevator button again. "Go back to Bronson. Know that I'm with Jax and everything is fine."

But everything wasn't fine.

Nothing was fine.

They weren't ever going to figure this out, were they?

They were just going to keep getting it wrong.

"Why did you come?" she whispered. "Why bring me a snack and clothes and a toothbrush?"

"Because you needed them." He stepped into the elevator, the doors closed and he was gone.

Logan spent the night in a recliner in Bronson's room. She dozed off and on, wanting to be available should Bronson wake up, but he didn't wake again until morning, and she stepped out as the doctors and nurses made their rounds and did what they needed to do.

Her hair had come down and she felt tired and disheveled but grateful Bronson was getting such excellent care.

He would be all right. He would be.

She used the visitor restroom to wash her face and brush her teeth and try to wake up. She craved coffee but didn't want to go all the way to the hospital cafeteria. Eventually she'd need to leave to see Jax and shower but she'd return. Hopefully her sisters could come soon, too, so Bronson would know he was loved and supported. It was time for the family to come together and be a proper family again. She loved them. All of them. Her mother. Bronson. Her sisters. Jax.

Rowan.

A lump filled her throat.

Lovers to adversaries—but maybe they could be friends. Maybe they could find a way to get along for Jax's sake. There was no reason they couldn't figure this out.

She stepped out of the ladies' room to discover Rowan standing guard outside Bronson's door. The nurses were still with Bronson, changing bandages and linens.

Her pulse jumped when she spotted Rowan and kept pounding as she walked toward him.

"Thought you might like this," he said, handing her a tall paper cup. "With milk and just enough sugar."

She'd thought she'd wanted coffee, but now that he was here, she only wanted him. Gorgeous, horrible, awful, wonderful Rowan Argyros. "Thank you," she said, accepting the cup while wishing he'd hug her instead.

She felt so sad. All night she'd been so sad. Why couldn't they make it work?

"How is everything?" he asked.

She glanced through the observation window to her brother. "He slept all night," she said. "The doctors seemed pleased earlier."

"That's good news."

She nodded. She struggled to find the words that would move them forward. Or back. Or to whatever place they needed to be so she could be close to Rowan again. She loved being close to Rowan. She'd never felt safer than when in his arms.

But Bronson had seen them and was struggling to sit up.

Logan shot Rowan an intense, searching look before turning away to enter Bronson's room.

"Don't do that," Logan said, moving to the side of her brother's bed and gently pressing him back. "Save your energy for getting better, not for entertaining us."

"But I do feel better already," he answered, his voice still raspy but significantly steadier than yesterday.

"You sound better," Rowan agreed, standing next to Logan. "And I know the police want to ask you more questions, but they're waiting until you're stronger. I've told them they need to give you time. They have a suspect in custody and he's confessed to shooting you, even though you were in the process of writing him a check."

"He really confessed?" Logan asked.

Rowan nodded. "He blames Daniel and Bronson for the collapse of his marriage and other problems."

"He didn't understand that Bronson was trying to pay Dad's clients back?"

Rowan shrugged. "Over 63 percent of your father's clients have been reimbursed, not from Bronson, but from money the government was able to seize from offshore accounts your father established. Bronson has been working on paying the remaining clients back, but it's taking him a while and many of those clients need money now, not in the future."

"It's true," Bronson said unsteadily. "I get letters daily from clients who have nothing—they lost everything. They're hurting. They've lost their retirement money, and the seniors have nothing else. They're old and vulnerable, and because of Father they're losing their homes." His voice was rough. "I've been getting these letters for years and every time I get one, I wire money and try to cover the bills. But no matter how much I send, there are still hundreds of people who need help."

"Dad embezzled the money, Bronson, not you."

"But I'm a Copeland. I couldn't live with myself if I didn't try to make amends."

"But you've worn yourself out."

"I'm not a victim. I won't play the victim."

She took his hand and held it tightly. "Bronson, you weren't the one who hurt those people—"

"It doesn't matter. I accept responsibility—"

"And so do I," Rowan said, interrupting. "It's my turn to help. You've done enough. I've spoken with Drakon and Mikael, too. We are taking over, and we will make sure the rest of your father's clients receive restitution."

Logan's jaw dropped. "Are you serious?"

Again Bronson struggled to rise. "That's not necessary—"

"But it is." Rowan's deep voice was flat and unemotional. "We have the ability to do this for the family, and we want to."

Bronson sagged back against the pillows. Logan just stared at Rowan. "Why would you do this?" she whispered.

He shrugged. "Because I can, and I want to."

"That doesn't make sense." She was truly baffled. "You hate my father. You hate him so much—"

"But I love you so much more."

Logan's lips parted but no sound came out. She stared up at Rowan, not just bewildered but overwhelmed.

"I grew up without money," he added, "and I've discovered that money can make life easier. It buys things and gives one the ability to do things, but it doesn't buy happiness, and it doesn't buy love. I would rather give away what I have, and help the people I love, than sit on a fortune and let you and your family suffer."

She blinked back tears. "You love us."

"Yes."

She rose and moved into his arms. "You really love us?" she repeated, even more urgently than before.

"Yes, *mo chroí*, I've been trying to tell you that for days."

"But you never used those words!"

"I told you that you were home."

"But *home* doesn't mean love—" She broke off, hearing herself, and made a soft, hoarse sound. "But it should, shouldn't it?"

"Yes." And then he was kissing her, and they forgot about Bronson until he made a rough sound and they broke apart, embarrassed but also laughing.

"So, you are friends," Bronson said with a faint smile.

Rowan looked at Logan, a brow arched.

Blushing, smiling, she nodded. "Yes." And then she moved back into Rowan's arms and whispered. "I love you. You know that, don't you? I've loved you from the moment I first laid eyes on you."

He grinned. "And you thought it was just great sex," he said huskily, voice pitched so low that only she could hear him.

And then he was pulling her out into the hallway to kiss her again. And again. And again.

"Marry me, *mo chroi*," he murmured against her mouth. "Marry me, please. I need you with me. I want you with me. Tell me you'll come home with me, please."

"Yes." She smiled up into his eyes. "Yes, yes, yes!"

# EPILOGUE

THEY WAITED THREE MONTHS to marry because Logan insisted that Bronson be the one to walk her down the aisle, and he needed time to recover.

The three months also gave them a chance to plan the wedding so that it wasn't a rushed affair, but the wedding of a lifetime.

After receiving her invitation, Victoria had at first sent her regrets, citing an unfortunate work commitment, but in the end every Copeland was there, flying to Ireland to attend the intimate ceremony at Castle Ros.

They were married at twilight in the castle's chapel with dozens of tall, ivory candles glowing at the front of the church, with more candles on each of the stone windowsills. The flickering candlelight illuminated the stained glass and the dramatic Gothic arches that formed the ceiling.

Logan wore an off-white silk gown that Jax picked out because Jax was the expert on princess gowns. The bridal gown's bodice was fitted through the waist and then turned into a huge bustled skirt.

The gown had needed last-minute alterations because the snug bodice became too snug. Logan was indeed pregnant, with twins.

She and Rowan had elected not to find out the sex, and

they were waiting until after the wedding to share the news with the rest of the family.

They'd tell Jax first, of course, because this had been her wish after all.

Logan's wish was that the babies would be healthy.

Rowan said he had no wishes because they'd all come true already. He had his wife—his *m' fhiorghra* or true love—his babies and his family, and he was referring to the Copelands as his family, too.

And so the beautiful candlelight wedding ceremony marked the end of the scandalous Copelands and the beginning of the happily-ever-after Copelands, as each of them moved forward with hope and love.

* * * * *

*If you enjoyed the final part of Jane Porter's*
THE DISGRACED COPELANDS,
*why not explore the first two installments?*

*THE FALLEN GREEK BRIDE*
*HIS DEFIANT DESERT QUEEN*

*Available now!*

# MILLS & BOON®

# MODERN™

**POWER, PASSION AND IRRESISTIBLE TEMPTATION**

0617/01

# MILLS & BOON®

## *EXCLUSIVE EXTRACT*

Ariston Kavakos makes impoverished Keeley Turner a
proposition: a month's employment on his island, at his
command. Soon her resistance to their sizzling chemistry
weakens! But when there's a consequence, Ariston makes
one thing clear: Keeley *will* become his bride…

*Read on for a sneak preview of*
### THE PREGNANT KAVAKOS BRIDE

'You're offering to *buy* my baby? Are you out of your
mind?'

'I'm giving you the opportunity to make a fresh start.'

'Without my *baby*?'

'A baby will tie you down. I can give this child
everything it needs,' Ariston said, deliberately allowing his
gaze to drift around the dingy little room. 'You cannot.'

'Oh, but that's where you're wrong, Ariston,' Keeley
said, her hands clenching. 'You might have all the houses
and yachts and servants in the world, but you have a great
big hole where your heart should be—and therefore you're
incapable of giving this child the thing it needs more than
anything else!'

'Which is?'

'Love!'

Ariston felt his body stiffen. He loved his brother and
once he'd loved his mother, but he was aware of his limi-
tations. No, he didn't do the big showy emotion he suspected
she was talking about and why should he, when he knew
the brutal heartache it could cause? Yet something told him
that trying to defend his own position was pointless. She

would fight for this child, he realised. She would fight with all the strength she possessed, and that was going to complicate things. Did she imagine he was going to accept what she'd just told him and play no part in it? Politely dole out payments and have sporadic weekend meetings with his own flesh and blood? Or worse, no meetings at all. He met the green blaze of her eyes.

'So you won't give this baby up and neither will I,' he said softly. 'Which means that the only solution is for me to marry you.'

He saw the shock and horror on her face.

'But I don't want to marry you! It wouldn't work, Ariston—on so many levels. You must realise that. Me, as the wife of an autocratic control freak who doesn't even like me? I don't think so.'

'It wasn't a question,' he said silkily. 'It was a statement. It's not a case of *if* you will marry me, Keeley—just when.'

'You're mad,' she breathed.

He shook his head. 'Just determined to get what is rightfully mine. So why not consider what I've said, and sleep on it and I'll return tomorrow at noon for your answer—when you've calmed down. But I'm warning you now, Keeley—that if you are wilful enough to try to refuse me, or if you make some foolish attempt to run away and escape…' he paused and looked straight into her eyes '…I will find you and drag you through every court in the land to get what is rightfully mine.'

*Don't miss*
THE PREGNANT KAVAKOS BRIDE
by Sharon Kendrick

Available July 2017
www.millsandboon.co.uk

33